WHERE THIS LAKE IS

WHERE THIS LAKE IS

JEFF LODGE

WHITE PINE PRESS • FREDONIA, NEW YORK

Publication of this book was made possible, in part, by grants from the New York State Council on the Arts and the National Endowment for the Arts.

Book Design: Elaine LaMattina

ISBN 1-877727-68-7

Printed and bound in the United States of America.

9 8 7 6 5 4 3 2 1

First Edition

Published by White Pine Press
10 Village Square
Fredonia, New York 14063

In memory of my grandparents,
Charles and Dorothy Glasco

CONTENTS

PART 1

PART 2

Part I

It was a deed of prophecy. As the moral gloom of the world overpowers all systematic gayety, even so was their home of wild mirth made desolate amid the sad forest.
—Nathaniel Hawthorne
"The Maypole of Merry Mount"

My life began
when I was born.
Hold the phone
I'll eat some corn.
—Maira Kalman
Max Makes a Million

Chapter I
Dear Diary, So to Speak

I'm not the man I used to be. But then, to paraphrase Mark Twain or maybe Will Rogers or some graffiti scrawled above a urinal in an I-70 rest stop just west of Columbus, Ohio—I never was. Let my life so far be a lesson to you, if you have any doubts or pretensions about what things are versus what they appear to be. Things *aren't* what they appear to be. This includes you.

For example, I live in Guatemala now. I own a restaurant in Tela, a town a few miles off the Pan-American Highway and adjacent to Lake Atitlán. The lake is glorious but dirty, polluted by sewage from the fifteen hundred or so people who live here, and from the natives who grow coffee in the hills above us.

The view from our shore brings tears of joy and wonder to the eyes. But during times when rain doesn't wash out the air, the lake smells a rotting-vegetable kind of ripe.

My restaurant is neither glorious nor dirty. It's only one room with a ten-seat, horseshoe shaped bar and a kitchen in the back. Pictures, some more well-composed than others, line its walls. Almost all are of me with my arm or arms around German or French or Canadian or American tourists, all of us grinning like idiots, one or all of us toasting the camera with a Guatemalan beer—a Moza, a Gallo, or a Monte Carlo.

I'm known as a friendly kind of guy here, gregarious.

The ceiling is a patchwork of thatched reeds, corrugated tin, and bulging sheetrock. The reeds come from the lake, the tin from the shed formerly behind the Hotel Tela, and the sheetrock from that same hotel's interior walls. When terrorists blew the place up in 1984, the rubbish just lay there for more than a year. Finally I figured if no one else was going to make use of the materials, I might as well. The guerrillas who blew it up shouldn't mind. They must have been wanting to say something about—how might they put it?—let's say, capitalist exploitation of their own people. And of their country's resources. For the pleasure of the idle rich. That's close enough.

I could use the stuff to roof my restaurant, and while maybe I served those idle rich, certainly I exploited them, too: five *quetzales*—a buck—for a bottle of beer. I only pay a dime apiece for them.

A lesson of my life. Some people might consider an American who owns his own business in a Central American country to be something of a sophisticate, a sort of world traveler. Until ten years ago, I'd never been more than twenty miles outside of Aiken, Ohio. So, I used to be a backwards hick, and now I'm not? Not likely, any way you look at it.

Until ten years ago I owned and ran what you might call a "general store" back in Aiken. I had taken it over from my father, who had taken it from his grandfather, who had inherited it from his father, and so on, clear back from 1822. That was the year my ancestor, George Wythe Hopkins, had heard the government was going to be building canals to connect Lake Erie with the Ohio River, and I guess had simply seen an opportunity to make a buck. From what I've been able to gather from the journals, now, looking for that opportunity in a specific sort of way hadn't really been an obsession for him, not consciously. Rather I think he was just a misfit, and he must have known intuitively that in some sense, the world of the new United States held nothing for him.

George Wythe's new life in what was then mostly wilderness must have been tough. Here is his second ever journal entry:

12 June, 1822
We have chosen well, with God's help. We have a stream for Water which runs deep and quick. Squirrels and rabbits are present in abundance. We have seen deer drink from the stream of the morning. We will have food and Prosper, with God's Help.

We sleep now in a shelter as those we built with Burr on Blennerhasset, but I have begun the foundation for what will be our House. Rocks are plentiful near the stream banks, within a walking distance I will have all the diverse I need. But Progress is slow, for of the children only three are able to help, and rain has filled the week since our arrival.

Jane has chosen an area for her garden, and when the rain quits I will burn it clear. It contains only one Chestnut, which I will first remove to use in the walls of the House. Of the House, Chestnuts are abundant, both green and seasoned. I believe I have brought the proper implements. The extra froes will be needed for splitting and riving. Must be careful of rot.

Of Jane, I have chosen well, with God's Help, for she is a strong woman, and she cares well for the baby and her family. If she cries she properly keeps it from us.

In His Faith,
George Wythe Hopkins

Two things strike me about this second-ever entry.

First, it provides clear evidence that George Wythe Hopkins was self-educated. Until I reached my teens and started to read real literature from his time, Hawthorne and Irving and others, I thought everybody in the nineteenth century wrote this way, using adjectives for nouns, capitalizing words at random. Maybe George Wythe could have written in a more normal style if he'd wanted to, maybe not. Maybe he simply fancied himself a poet when he was anything but. Either way, he sure screwed up my concept of English for a while.

Doing it yourself doesn't always work.

Second thing that strikes me, the man talked as if he thought he was constructing a new Eden in his backwoods frontier. If only he could have seen the Aiken that Audrey and I left behind, ten years ago now.

Audrey was my wife. She was a strong woman too, like George Wythe's Jane Wolcott Aiken, the woman for whom his and my now-dead town was named. When I want to think fondly of Audrey now, I remember her in the days we were packing to leave. She usually kept her back to me, facing the bare walls. Speaking brought staccato echoes. Her hair was mostly gray, though she, like me, was only thirty at the time, and it sloped into a plastic, usually tortoise-shell barrette that hung a few inches below her shoulders, it then dropped hugging the curve of her back nearly to her waist. I liked her back, the nicely crooked, incomplete vee it formed from her broad shoulders down to her slight waist.

From behind, I watched her hands as she packed the green Ohio-shaped ashtrays, glossy green with blue squiggly lines representing rivers and canals. They were going back to Freyse, not coming with us. Thick-veined hands, the hands of a woman who worked hard, not only for herself, but for her husband, too. Rough-looking hands, but deceptively smooth from the cream she used on them every night. I was never sure whether she did that for me or for herself.

We should have talked more.

Packing. The driver from Freyse, my primary wholesaler, came the Thursday before the Friday Audrey and I left Aiken. He took everything but the perishables, meat and cheese and the like. Before he left, he wrote out a check for what he was taking, fifty cents on the dollar minus transportation costs. I didn't know if that was a standard deal in the business or not—the store had only been mine for a couple of years—but I didn't feel in a position to negotiate for something better.

About the journals. The journals are the Hopkins family's family albums, so to speak. George Wythe began them the day he reached what would become Aiken in 1822. Later his son kept them, then five other Hopkins men chosen either by fate or by their fathers for the task. My father died eleven years ago, and the journals and their responsibility became mine the day he died.

Here is my first entry:

> *May 5, 1981*
> *Father died today. Father, Thomas Jefferson Hopkins II. I'll miss him, but now I have to do all this goddamned writing.*
> *Jerry Hopkins*

When Audrey and I left Aiken, I stopped keeping the journals. They were the history both of the Hopkins family, as I said, and of Aiken itself. Aiken was dead, though. We were the last to leave. And our son hadn't been born yet, and it looked like he wasn't going to be. The family was running smack into a genetic dead end.

I started again two years later, in Tucson, about the time our son Moses came along. Still, I don't write in them much. This, what I'm writing now, may eventually end up in them. I haven't decided yet. I just feel like writing down some things. I'm not sure the journals are the place for them.

Another lesson:

In the summer of 1984, a couple of years after Audrey and I left Aiken, we were working at the Flying Z, a ranch in the Laramie Mountains of eastern Wyoming. She did the books, and I irrigated, cut, then baled hay, flood-irrigated, very primitive and exhausting. Johnny Proctor raised Appaloosas on the next ranch south. His place was only sixteen hundred acres (ours—or, more precisely, Henry Chilcutt's—was thirty thousand), but I guess he made an okay living. He was engaged to Robin Chilcutt, Boss Henry's fat daughter.

"Movin' into the big house," Johnny used to say.

One afternoon in August, Johnny and I were sitting on the planked porch of that big house, drinking Coors while our sweat evaporated and left our skin gritty. Fun times on the range. Henry Chilcutt always kept a keg of Coors around. A regional thing, I guess.

"Jerry," Johnny Proctor said, "there's only two kinds of people." That didn't seem likely to me. Since I'd left Aiken, I'd seen white folks, black folks, hispanics down in Denver. I'd seen rich folks and poor folks and people somewhere in the big middle. And I knew some people were nice and caring, and some were just outright mean. But Johnny usually amused me, so I humored him.

"Give 'em to me," I said. A quick wind brought the odor of horse manure.

"You got your poets." He took a swig of beer. "And you got your mechanics."

"Poets and mechanics," I said, thinking his words sounded profound, though maybe it was the beer and the heat. Whatever, I think I believed them, and since then I've returned to them whenever things, and people, have seemed to be getting too complicated.

Three people work for me here in Tela:

Carmela, an Indian woman—Cackchiquel, I think—cooks breakfast and makes soups. In the mornings the restaurant smells strongly and wonderfully of garlic and cilantro and spices whose names and fragrances I don't know. She also keeps the stray dogs and cats out of the kitchen. With her long wooden spoons, she's the Joe DiMaggio of Central American female cooks. I pay her fifty *quetzales* a week—about ten bucks—and I give her Mondays off. The guy that owned Daddy Rabbit's before me only paid her twenty-five, and he made her work every day.

The guerrillas should be proud of me.

Gonzalo cooks dinners and closes the place up, translates for me when I need it, and fixes anything that goes wrong. He also keeps my restaurant from smelling of stale beer—remember I told you it was neither glorious *nor* dirty—with his mops and his rags and his soap. Gonzalo put the ceiling together. Johnny Proctor would probably call him a mechanic. I pay him fifty *quetzales* a week too, but I let him take leftovers home, maybe to his family, but maybe not. He might be Carmela's brother-in-law or something. She's the one that brought him to me, back when I first bought the place.

Nati, she's about twenty-three, twenty-four now, tends bar when I don't, which is most of the time. She keeps my house clean as well, but I only pay her forty *quetzales* a week. I give her a place to sleep, though, and I buy her clothes and jewelry when she asks me, sometimes when she doesn't. She always smells pleasantly of flowers, honeysuckle maybe, shades of yellow sprinkling green and sweetly edible. Nati doesn't have a family—they were all slaughtered across the lake, in San Pedro la Laguna, by the civil patrols a few years ago. Her brother had been seen talking to a known rebel.

That's a hundred-forty *quetzales* a week I pay for labor. A little extra for Gonzalo, a little extra for Nati. Twenty-five, thirty beers. On a Friday night, when the rich *ladinos* from Guatemala City hit town, I sell that many in half an hour.

That I don't tell to the guerrillas.

The journals again. It bothers me sometimes that I don't seem to show the reverence for them that the men before me seemed to, but some things are just hard to change. Assuming that this new writing doesn't make it into them, here is my latest entry:

July 4, 1992
They're celebrating up north today. Whoopie! We're free.
Gerard Manley Hopkins

Despite my name, I'm pretty sure I don't fall into the poet category. If I ever see young Moses, he can take over.

CHAPTER II
IT'TH GOD, TALKING TO YOU

God can just go to hell. When I was a kid and still had friends and still lived in Aiken, I decided that was the worst thing a person could say. The Saturday me and Audrey abandoned Aiken, we went to the cemetery first. It surrounded the church that sat on the county road to Ankneytown, a few hundred yards off the main highway. Our last pastor, Brother Jarvis, had left two years earlier, and now most of the windows were broken out and the whitewash where it wasn't peeling had faded to gray. It looked as if to touch it would bring splinters. A For Sale sign, new, of Jack Bracken, Jr., greeted us.

God can just go to hell, I thought.

But he sent us there first.

From the time I was nine or ten or so, I took care of the cemetery. I'd mow it with the pushmower, hand-trim around the headstones, pull weeds. Later, after we were married, Audrey told me she used to watch me sometimes. I'd never known that.

"You seemed possessed," she said. "Crazy. Like a crazy old man in a boy's body."

"A guy's got to have something to do," I said. And if he's going to do something, he might as well do it right, I thought. Those were my father's words. By way, no doubt, of my grandfather Tom, a self-styled poet if ever there was one.

The cemetery. Its headstones started at the east side of the base of the church's steps, with the marker of George Wythe Hopkins, 1787-1863, and the smaller stone of his wife, Jane Wolcott Aiken Hopkins. Then they traveled around the south side forming a sort of semi-circle. The ones I remember best are these:

Benjamin Harrison Hopkins, 1825-1898 (son of George);
Francis Lightfoot Lee Hopkins, 1847-1898 (the first son of Benjamin; the two, father and son, had died together in a horse-and-buggy runaway);
Carter Braxton Hopkins, 1869-1935 (first son of Francis);
Thomas Nelson Hopkins II, 1898-1963 (the only son of Carter);
Thomas Jefferson Hopkins, 1924-1981 (my father and the only son of Thomas Nelson II).

Every time I saw the headstones, and when I think of them now, I think, from the journals, of two other men not represented there. There had been a Richard Henry Lee Hopkins, buried in Chattanooga after Missionary Ridge, if you know anything about the Civil War; and a Thomas Nelson Hopkins (not the father of the second, but the uncle) buried in Cuba during the Spanish-American War. Nobody ever really said—not in the journals, and not my father directly—but I gathered that Thomas Nelson died of syphilis.

A real war hero, my ancestor.

If your antebellum American history is any good, you might have noticed that all of the above were named after the seven Virginia signers of the Declaration of Independence. By the time my turn had come, though, all the names had been used up, as well as most of the seconds and thirds. I got stuck with the name of a poet.

Just after dawn the Friday before Audrey and I deserted Aiken, the man from Sunoco showed up at the store to pick up the gasoline I hadn't sold. He stood in the fog on the porch and smoked a cigarette while the gasoline moved up through the tubing from the underground tank into his tanker. He held out his pack to me, and I shook my head no. Fire and fumes don't mix all that well, and though I felt depressed—who wouldn't?—I hadn't yet become suicidal.

He smelled thickly of grease, gasoline, and oil, and he told me about an antique dealer up in Loudonville who might be interested in the pumps.

"I think I better leave 'em," I said. I'd never thought of the pumps, forties vintage that needed to be primed before each use, as antiques. They were just something else that had always been around. "You never know," I said. "We might come back." He wrote something on a piece of paper and handed it to me.

"Case you change your mind," he said. I took the piece of paper, glanced at it without the letters and numbers registering, and shoved it into my hip pocket.

I said I didn't think I'd change my mind.

I haven't yet. As far as I know the pumps are still there, and I still own them.

The Lubbers place sat across the highway from the pumps and the store, probably still does, and the ditch that used to be the canal formed its back property line. Percy Lubbers had moved his family to Florida the week of Thanksgiving, 1978. Nothing left in Aiken to give thanks for, I guess.

The branches of four weeping willows hung over the ditch. As boys, Stevie Lubbers and I used to camp out beneath them. We'd pretend we were American soldiers, in France, maybe, fighting the Germans across the canal. We'd lob fist-sized rocks into the trees on its far side and pretend they were hand grenades.

Audrey liked those willows. Once after my father died she asked if we could buy the Lubbers place. I'd only had a few days to go over my father's books, but I'd seen enough to know we didn't have any spare cash and we weren't going to any time soon. I had to say no.

"Can't do it," I said that day. "Sorry."

"Oh," she said. I think it crushed her.

Here, from my namesake, is a verse, a sonnet:

"Not, I'll not, carrion comfort, Despair, not feast on thee,
Not untwist—slack they may be—these last strands of man
In me ór, most weary, cry, I can no more. I can;
Can something, hope, wish day come, not choose to be.

But ah, but O thou terrible, why wouldst thou rude on me
Thy wring-world right foot rock? lay a lionlimb against me? scan
With darkness devouring eyes my bruisèd bones? and fan,
O in turns of tempest, me heaped there; me frantic to avoid
      thee and flee?

Why? That my chaff might fly; my grain lie, sheer and clear.
Nay in all that toil, that coil, since (seems) I kissed the rod,
Hand rather, my heart lo! lapped strength, stole joy, would
      laugh, chéer.
Cheer whom though? The Hero whose heaven-handling flung
      me, fóot tród
Me? or me that fought him? O which one? is it each one? That
      night, that year
Of now done darkness I wretch lay wrestling with (my God!)
      my God."

Now *there* was a poet! And I'm not so sure that what he had to say about God was all that different from what me and Stevie had to say.

Some more about God.

After Aiken, then after Granville, Audrey and I lived for a bit in Columbus. We found a cheap apartment on the near east side just off Bryden Road. From what we understood, the complex had been built in the forties for employees of St. Ann's Hospital; only a line of trees separated us from the hospital.

Norma was our next door neighbor. She worked at the hospital, in housekeeping, had one upper tooth and no lowers, and owned a dog whose feet, she seemed proud to say, had never touched the ground. The dog shit and pissed on newspaper in her kitchen. She thought it was housebroken.

Norma talked a lot, and her stories scared Audrey and made me nervous.

"Hoodlumth in the neighborhood," she'd say. "No rethpect. They'll thteal your truck." Or, "Look out for the ratth. They come up through the toiletth." Or, "The woman who uthed to live in your apartment wath found dead. Thtabbed thirty timeth."

One day I asked her this: "How long have you lived here Norma?"

"Twenty-four yearth now."

"And when were the rats?"

"The latht time wath nineteen thickthty-two, if I recollect right."

She didn't have to scare us like that, no, she didn't.

We had vicious and fickle water pressure in that apartment. During the course of a fifteen-minute shower, the temperature would change from hot to scalding to cold and back a dozen times. One morning, over coffee and doughnuts in Norma's kitchen, we asked her if she had the same problem. Her apartment smelled ripe like a pig farm, and her little orange rat-faced dog, Red, lay asleep at my feet under the table.

"It'th not a problem," she said. "It'th God, talking to you."

"God?" Audrey said.

"God. The Holy Thpirit. He's got to have thome way to communicate." Red got up, sniffed the table leg, then walked the two steps to his newspaper and let go a whizz.

"God," I said.

Talking to you.

I wasn't keeping my end of the family journal bargain at the time, but if I had been, I might have included the following in that day's entry:

You can't choose your neighbors.

Sometime around dusk of the Friday before the Saturday Audrey and I turned our backs on Aiken, we finished loading the pick-up. After I tightened the tarp over the load, we took a couple of sleeping bags and a flashlight across the highway to the Lubbers place. We walked down the driveway with the leg-tickling knee-high weeds running down the ridge of its center, then past the house and the garage, both out of view from the highway but still boarded up against vandals. The boards had become rotted over the last couple of years. In the half-light behind the house, I noticed six posts, wire strung between them, that had once held Stevie's mother's grape arbors. Two posts, decayed at their bases, had fallen over—one to the ground, the other held at an odd angle by the pull of the wires. Stevie and I used to snitch grapes from the arbors. His mother, when she'd catch us, would holler, maybe threaten Stevie with a switch, but it was worth it. I tried to remember how the grapes had tasted, but only a mustiness came, like beets, or the smell of a basement.

I thought then I'd be glad to get the hell out.

Me and Audrey picked a spot beneath the willows just a few feet from the ditch. I cleared out a couple of rocks—just rocks, not grenades—and we spread out the sleeping bags. In the smell of stagnant water still standing from the last rain, amid the sawing of crickets, swatting away occasional mosquitoes, and beneath the canopy formed by the trees' branches and backlit by a half moon that sporadically split the clouds, we made love our last night in Aiken.

She was hot, on fire. So was I.

I thought the night romantic, but what did I know?

We woke up sometime around dawn, if we'd even fallen asleep, and with the sky beginning blue, we crouched ankle-deep and naked in the mud beside the ditch. Without speaking, we used the warm, scummed water to rinse off our mingled fluids. We dressed, then still in silence headed for the cemetery.

Another word about where Audrey and I were at the time, about Aiken, about Aiken and leaving it:

When I was a teenager, our town still had a school, three rooms: one for grades one through six, one for seven through nine, and one for ten through twelve. The teachers might have had a fourth room for their office, but I never knew. I always behaved myself. By the mid-seventies, when I was in my early twenties, the school closed down for lack of students. The few families who were still around sent their kids down Highway 13 to Mount Vernon.

But those of us who before that went to the school had taken, in the seventh and eighth grades, Ohio history and geography. I learned that Ohio, before the settlers and before my ancestor George Wythe Hopkins, had been populated by the Moundbuilders, the Hopewell Indians. I think they were the same people, the Moundbuilders and the Hopewells. And they probably had a third name, the name they called themselves. If I had an encyclopedia around now I'd look it up to make sure. My part-time next-door neighbor here in Tela, Miguel Romero (I say part-time because he spends a good deal of his days at another house, a country *villa* south of Tela), Miguel has a set of encyclopedias. Britannicas, I think. When I go over for drinks on an occasional evening I always notice them, the only books in his house as far as I know, displayed probably proudly—otherwise why the show?—on a shelf in the foyer just before you get to the gun rack.

Miguel's encyclopedias are written in Spanish, though, and I might speak it well enough to get by, especially if I have my man Gonzalo to help me over the rough spots, but I can't read it for shit.

The guerrillas, if they knew, probably wouldn't appreciate that, that American arrogance.

Back to Aiken. Once, when I was in the seventh or eighth grade, my teacher—I don't remember her name—scheduled a field trip for us. We were going to visit the Indian mounds in Newark, a city, still alive today, about forty miles south of Aiken. She was going to drive us, all nine of us, in her station wagon. She had a heart attack the day before, though, and we never went. The next day, the day of our scheduled trip, Mr. Melvin, the high school teacher, told us Miss What's-her-name had spent the night in intensive care at Newark's Licking County Memorial Hospital. She had died early that morning.

I remember thinking that some people get all the luck.

At least she had gotten to go to Newark.

Gonzalo, by the way, didn't show up for work today. Not to clean or cook or translate or anything else. I'll have to ask Carmela about him.

We learned our Ohio history there in the seventh and eighth grades, but as I said we learned our geography too. Ohio, we were taught, was bordered by Lake Erie on the north and the Ohio River on the south. Some smaller rivers flowed into the lake, some into the Ohio, and in the nineteenth century some canals, one of which was right outside the school building, had been built to connect the two great bodies of water.

I already knew that, though, about the canals. I had the journals. I needed to know more, about Ohio, about America, about the world.

I was an inquisitive sort.

One day, one rainy day, I asked my father where the rain went.

"Just seeps into the ground," he said. "Refills the aquifer."

"No," I said. "I mean when the ground gets full and it can't take any more."

"The runoff, you mean."

"Okay," I said. I could be patient with my father.

"Into the creek there," he said. "Into Aiken's Run."

We were sitting on the store's sheltered porch, in the two comfortable wooden rockers, and I turned towards him as he spoke. I got a whiff of his breath, decaying teeth or whiskey, then turned back away. "Then where?" I said to the road.

"Into the Walhonding, and then the Muskingum." My father could be patient with me too, I guess.

"Where does it stop?" I said.

"I suppose it doesn't. Goes into the Ohio, the Mississippi, and then the Gulf of Mexico, down by New Orleans." My geography hadn't gotten me out of Ohio yet. I didn't know where New Orleans was, at least not exactly. "Goes from being fresh water, water you can drink," he said, "to salt water. It's natural."

The whole process might have been, might be, a natural thing. I wanted to believe that, Christ, I want to believe it even now. My father was smart. He knew everything. But I couldn't help but wonder why, when they were all so connected, bodies of water were given different names. So when a person was next to one, he would know where he was?

I'm next to Lake Atitlán in Guatemala. If I walk outside my restaurant and into the road, then look southwest, I can see it, the lake. I can see the fishing boats tied to the rotting piers on its shore, the flat reflective expanse that might be fifteen miles or a thousand between our shore and the far one, the two triangular volcanoes that grow from beyond that far shore and dwarf the lake and any sense I might want to have that the life of a little speck of a person has any meaning whatsoever beyond, beyond slinging beers and being a friendly kind of guy and paying the help a decent wage and having enough left over to send some back to Moses, seven now, in Arizona, and enough time as well as enough money, enough time to make up for the thirty or so years wasted in Aiken, Ohio, living the lives of a century and a half of Hopkins men, living my own life but not living my own life.

I'm next to Lake Atitlán now, in Guatemala, but where am I?

Sometimes still I think this:

God help me.

CHAPTER III
HIS KIND OF WOMAN

My father was born in 1924, a hundred and two years after George Wythe Hopkins first came to Aiken. He was the youngest of his parents' three children, and his mother, my grandmother Dorothy, had a hard time during his delivery. Jeannette Lubbers from across the road, Percy's mother, handled the whole thing, being trained during World War I as a nurse, and thus able to act as mid-wife.

My father was a breech baby, ornery even before he could breathe by himself. Dorothy screamed, they thought she was going to die, my father turned blue, they thought he was going to die, then Dorothy screamed and turned blue herself. This happened several times over several hours, but with Jeannette Lubbers's hands up inside her roughly then gently then roughly turning my father in the right direction, she finally squeezed him out.

My great-grandfather, Carter Braxton Hopkins, kept the journals at that time. Here is part of the entry he made that day:

July 19, 1924

...I warned Tom about that woman...

C. B. H.

Young Tom, my father, must have known from some time near his beginning that life wouldn't always be easy. But it wouldn't always be hard, either. He grew up for a time during the twenties, then during the Depression of the thirties. Nobody mentioned it in the journals so I suppose the Depression might not have affected Aiken much. That'd be understandable, I suppose. Everybody lived mostly off what they grew, and my family lived mostly off them. The nuclear weapons plant up on Pleasant Hill Lake between Ankneytown and Loudonville, where some of Aiken's people would eventually work, hadn't been built yet, of course. And Ohio didn't experience any drought. Never does. If I had to imagine, I might imagine that prices for Aiken's excess might have dropped, and that the store's sales might have followed, but even if that happened, again nobody ever said.

Maybe they sold their leftovers to the government, which of course would always pay more for something than what it was worth, still does. Wouldn't surprise me, Roosevelt had so many programs going in those days. Maybe the Depression was even a boom time for Aiken.

"God bless America," my people might have said poetically in those days.

Times change, don't they.

The Depression might have passed us by, but the war, World War II, didn't. None of Aiken's people had ever seen any Japanese, and the notion that some little yellow folks from across the ocean that wrote backwards and thus couldn't be very bright would try to bully them pissed them off. My father, already over six feet tall and muscular like a draft horse, enlisted right after Pearl Harbor.

My grandfather had taken over the journals in 1934, the year before his father, Carter Braxton Hopkins, or C.B.H., died. He started the year before instead of right after because C.B.H. thought himself a mechanic. He was working on the engine of his truck when the hood suddenly slammed shut, snapping both his arms at the elbow. They had to come off.

My grandfather only had one arm, his left—he'd lost the other to gangrene in World War I—and though he'd been right-handed he had taught himself to write, to make do with what he had. That war experience seemed to give him a more reasonable perspective on the sense of trying to show some foreigner that America was the boss. In his portion of the journal he wrote this of my father:

August 24, 1942

Letter from young Tom today, dated three weeks ago. Censored, as usual, so again I don't know where he is. Or was, I should say. They must move a lot. In my war we stayed in one place, until we died or lost limbs, then we came home. Tom is younger now than I was then. The news today talks of ship movements in the Solomon Islands and a place called Savo.

Too many unfamiliar names. Like in France. Midway, Wake, New Caledonia, Papua, Château-Thierry, Saint-Mihiel, finally Compiègne. Tom is too young, at a month past eighteen, he shouldn't be there. None of our boys should. He's been promoted to radio, he says, says it like he's proud. No hint he's discovered that Roosevelt cares no more for him than Wilson did for us.

I spent a long while today sitting out back listening to the trains.

It rained.

More trains going north than south. To Mansfield, Marion, Galion, Ashland. Cleveland and Columbus have direct routes, more or less, from the coasts. I don't know what's in the boxes now, but soon enough we'll be in Europe and they'll be carrying boys back home, dead boys in boxes. Some husbands. Some fathers. Seeing them, their mothers and wives will cry, scream, and take their anger out on the Japs and the Germans instead of on our generals, those bastards—excuse me—that will have sent them to their deaths.

I pray again that young Tom will return home safe. But I know that even if his body makes it, his mind, his heart, will be changed forever. He will have seen death before him, and, as with me, he will have become hardened from it. He won't be able to love like he should, for who when they have lived face to face with their own mortality can look at the future with anything but despair?

Enough for today.

Thomas Nelson Hopkins II

That last is true, in a sense I suppose, but a bit melodramatic, isn't it? When he came home from his war, my father was able to love, at least enough to marry my mother, and to father four children, and to raise them without most of them coming to hate him. And though I might feel a despair from time to time, I'm pretty sure I didn't get it from him.

Wars. Other wars.

Audrey and I lived in Denver for a while, after Granville and Columbus and before Wyoming. We managed an apartment building on Corona Street, just south of that long dividing line of Colfax. The Huntington, the building was called, built in 1892 (when George Wythe's seventh child, Ben, was keeping the journals, incidentally), so said the engraving on the entrance's granite transom. It had twenty units, plus one for me and Audrey, and always smelled moldy like tomatoes left in the window too long, nothing you could do about it.

Norman Wright lived on the third floor, lived on disability from when he'd gotten a foot blown off in Vietnam. Though we had lived around some black folks back in Columbus, Norman was the first one I was ever really friends with. He always smiled, and we spent a good deal of time sitting on the noisy front porch drinking beers and talking about the crazy neighbors and him telling war stories and me listening—my father never spoke about his war. I don't know why. We even went skiing together once. He did pretty well, for a guy with only one foot.

Once Norman disappeared for a day, then two, then three, and Audrey and I got worried—we'd heard stories about flashbacks. We went looking, and found him in the nut ward at the Veterans Hospital. He didn't recognize us. His eyes were cloudy and dripping white and he shuffled while he walked, shuffled now on top of his hobble. Thorazine, he'd tell us later, smiling again.

Life can be hard sometimes, I learned. Hard enough that you've got to be careful, conscious of the least little thing. Like what war you decide you're going to be a part of, for example, like when you open your restaurant what you're going to call it.

When I bought the place here in Guatemala, it had been closed a year or more. But the sign, whitewashed plywood with black gloss lettering, still hung over the door. "MARIO'S," all caps, that was all. I didn't know what kind of baggage that name carried, what kind of word-of-mouth might have traveled between foreigners—journalists and the like—

who came down year after year then made their recommendations to anyone they sent our way. Not knowing, I decided to change the name. Safer that way. If the place would fail, it should be my fault, not that of my predecessor.

If you went a block and a half north from me and Audrey's apartment building in Denver, then took Colfax about two blocks west, toward downtown, you came to a block-long strip of businesses, all selling sex, all bearing the same name: Daddy Rabbit's Arcade, Videos 25¢; Daddy Rabbit's Lounge, Topless Dancers; Daddy Rabbit's Peep, Live Nude Girls; Daddy Rabbit's Art Theatre, First Run XXX. Most of our time in Denver, I worked across the street, and sometimes when I'd get off early I'd go visit one place or another. I never told Audrey that, but it wouldn't surprise me if she knew. I'm not a very good liar. The girls, women, who danced for us at the lounge or bared it all at the Peep drew me and puzzled me. Sometimes they'd kiss each other, on stage and off. They excited me and aroused me—of course, they were supposed to—but they made me think of my sister Jane.

But back to names. Remembering Denver, I chose Daddy Rabbit's as the name for my place here in Tela. Nobody'd make the connection, I figured. So far I've been right. And the pronunciation in English is close enough to the Spanish that if someone were to ask directions, looking for the place they'd heard of back in the states, they would be understood well enough to eventually find their way to come spend their money with me. The Spanish word for rabbit is *conejo*, and I suppose I could have used that when I named my restaurant, but what American could remember it?

I've made a few right choices here and there.

Jane.
I had three sisters. Still do, as far as I know. I'm the oldest of the four children. Jane, the youngest, hated our father right up until he died. Then she made a show of crying at the funeral.

Our father.
Mount Vernon, seven or eight miles down Highway 13 from Aiken, used to have one movie theater, the Esquire, downtown on Mansfield.

When I'd go there in the fifties and sixties it was already old, had a huge screen and a stage, a fancy chandelier, lights on the aisle seats, and ceiling-to-floor plush curtains lining all its walls. Until the late sixties, they charged adults fifty cents, children under twelve thirty-five.

In the summer of 1951, young Tom Hopkins and the woman who would be my mother, June Bracken, went to the Esquire for their first date. It cost a dime apiece, though certainly my father paid for both of them, and they saw *His Kind of Woman*, starring Robert Mitchum and Jane Russell.

My father, until he died, always reminded me of Robert Mitchum, tall and square-shouldered, muscular like a Cadillac, but no fins; my mother until I grew up reminded me of no one. I couldn't imagine what she might have looked like younger. I have a picture of her, though, one that I found a few years ago pressed like a leaf between a couple of pages of my father's sections of the journals. Odd it took me so long to find it. Her shoulders are bare and her hair flows long to rest on them. Her eyebrows are painted high and thin, and she's wearing a dark lipstick I never saw her wear in real life. The photo's black and white, so I don't know the color of the lipstick. With a different nose, one more Italian, you might say, my mother would have looked like Jane Russell.

I don't know if my parents-to-be enjoyed themselves at that movie. They never said. But at some point something must have clicked between them.

Six months later they made me.

Young Tom and June Bracken had met only a few weeks before that date. June's family was new to Aiken, from Cincinnati. They moved into the Melvin farm, just outside of town on the way to Amity. Harry Melvin was getting old, in his eighties, and he and his wife Thelma had only had one child, a boy who would one day be my school's high school teacher; he was away at Ohio U and would never marry, and they, Harry and Thelma, couldn't make the place work anymore.

The Brackens and the Melvins were related somehow, cousins, I think. June's family took over the farm, and Harry and Thelma moved into their place down in Cincinnati, better for folks their age. Young June met Tom in my family's store. My father told me of their meeting:

"I can't seem to find the shotgun shells," she said to him, her voice smooth like cat's fur.

"You're new here," my father said, his deep and hard like Robert Mitchum's, though certainly not from conscious effort.

"If I wasn't, would it be easier to find them?"

"Find what?" my father said. His mind was more on the striking new woman before him than on what she'd said.

"The shotgun shells."

"We keep them behind the counter. Going hunting?"

"My father is. Taking my brothers. They've never done it before. They're going to end up shooting each other."

"We got licenses too," my father said. Always looking to make an extra buck.

"Do they need them?" my mother said. He could tell she was from the city. If the men in her family didn't know the basics, they probably *would* end up shooting each other.

"What are they hunting?"

"Rabbits, I guess."

"I got rabbits in the back, frozen," he said. "Save them a lot of trouble."

"I'll tell them you said that."

"Tell them first, go now, and if they still want to do it themselves, come back and I'll sell you some shells and licenses."

"Thanks," my mother said.

"My pleasure," said my father. "I'll need to know what kind of shotguns they have, too."

"Remingtons, I think."

"No, what size."

"Oh."

And so forth. Their conversation seems now more poetic than mechanical.

I never met my wife Audrey, not the way my father met his wife. Like the canals, like my family's store, like the old gas pumps out front of it, she was just something else that was always around.

My mother's father and her brothers ended up going hunting that day, and her older brother Jack blew his right foot off. Although he tried for a couple of years, brother Jack couldn't very well be much help around the farm, having that bum leg and all. He moved down to Mount Vernon and eventually became a realtor. He got married and had seven kids, and named the oldest one Jack Jr. It was Jack Jr.'s name that was on all the For Sale signs that sprang up around Aiken in the late seventies and early eighties, in front of the Lubbers's place, the Brackens', and so forth, even the old church. Jack Jr. never got to slap the "Sold" signs across them, though, at least by the time Audrey and I left.

Life is full of disappointments.

Always thinking I might come back, I never let my cousin Jack Jr. put a sign out front of the store. Once a year I still send the county a check for taxes. In fact, they come due this month.

Excuse me.

I have to go sell some beers.

When my father died, it was from cancer. My mother died three years earlier, from cancer too. It seems a lot of people from Aiken had cancer in those days. Maybe we should have suspected that weapons plant earlier than we did.

My mother hung on for three months after her disease was diagnosed, my father for six. Both felt it in their shoulders first. It had gotten up into their bones there, then into their ribs, then everywhere. My mother died in Knox County Hospital. So did my father. He was pretty much unconscious the last week, medication for the pain. This was how the conversation between him and my sister Jane went, a week before he died, right before he went out for the last time:

"You killed your mother," he said, his voice not Robert Mitchum's, but rather a weak, raspy Vincent Price's through his yellowed oxygen mask. "Now you've killed me, too."

"You'll make it, Father," my sister Jane said.

"She didn't hear me," my father said in my direction. I was sitting on the opposite side of the bed from Jane. "You tell her." I looked at Jane, shrugged, and didn't say anything.

"You're being a shithead," Jane said to my father on his deathbed.

"You've always been a shithead."

"You're evil, Jane," my father said. "Of the devil."

"But I'm alive," she said.

I haven't always understood why my sister Jane hated my father, why they hated each other. This notion of causality confuses me sometimes. I want to believe, I guess, that what comes before determines what comes after, and not, at least once in awhile, that things happen the other way around. But somehow I know better.

Within three years of my birth, two of my sisters showed up—my parents were active. Then for some reason they stopped making babies until Jane came along ten years after me. She must have been an accident. But do I only think that now, after seeing what she's grown up to be? Or did I think that at the time, could I have thought that, before she'd had a chance to disrupt my family and bring feelings of hate into a house that hadn't known them before? Could even my father have thought her an accident when she was born? Or do I only remember those words from him later, after the two had grown to despise each other.

Today's Tuesday, and Gonzalo still hasn't shown up for work. I'm only a little worried, since he's done this before. He's probably doing his week of duty with the *patrullas civiles* (I'm practicing my *español*), the civil patrols. They're our local type of National Guard, you might say, only service in them is mandatory, not voluntary, especially for the Indians. Except for rare occasions, here in Tela you only see them at night, after hours—somewhere someone has warned them about bothering the tourists—when they pull into town laughing and drunk in their surplus American troop carriers, noisy enough to make you want to shake them and tell them to behave, though you don't. They have guns.

I thought again of asking Carmela about Gonzalo, I think they're related, but she's been busy chasing dogs out of the kitchen with her long wooden spoons.

I don't think she's in the mood for conversation.

Chapter IV
My Sisters Move Away

Jane is my youngest sister. As I've said, not the only one. Rachel is a year younger than me, Linda three. Rachel and Linda are both married, and they both have children. Unlike Jane, they both put their time in at the store, at least until their men came by and took them away.

Rachel's was a soldier-to-be from Chesterville, a few miles west, who in 1971 was on his way to Mount Vernon to volunteer for the army and Vietnam. He stopped at the store for gas. She took his money, and they talked for a long time. She was thin, but only in her waist and not too much so, reminds me now of the Jane Russell who I hadn't ever seen at that time. He had a crew-cut that showed a scar above his left ear, and these slanted eyebrows that jutted sharp-boned what seemed like inches out over his eyes. I was straightening up the magazines just a few feet away, and as they talked I couldn't help but listen. It was early autumn, and our mother was in the back, in her kitchen, canning snap beans. My father was over helping the Brackens, his in-laws, harvest their corn, probably showing them how to start up their combine.

"I've already talked to them once," Sid, my future first brother-in-law said. "After basic I'll go to Fort Bragg, in North Carolina. Then I'll get to go to Nam."

"Are you scared?" my sister said.

"Of course not. And somebody's got to defend this country."

"You played football, didn't you, in high school?" We didn't have a team there in Aiken, too small, but Rachel, still in school herself, followed the other teams in our part of the county. I don't know why.

"Quarterback, for Chesterville," he said. "You've heard of me?"

"Who hasn't?" my sister said. She was all starry-eyed, pissed me off, her falling so easy, if that was what she was doing.

On his way back from Mount Vernon and his recruiting officer, the Sid guy stopped again. Rachel was still behind the counter, and they talked again, again for a long time. I was stocking a shipment of motor oil and transmission fluid. Jane, nine then, tapped me on the shoulder.

"Who's the geek?" she said, precocious. I don't know where she got those words. You had to laugh.

"Nobody," I said. "Just some football player from over west."

"He's going to take her away from here, isn't he?"

"Well if he does," I said, "that just narrows your competition."

Jane, young as she was, got my joke and poked me in the ribs. "Fart on boys," she said. I thought she was cute then. What did I know?

"Wait till you get older," I said.

"No boys," she said. "Ever." And she stomped out the store's front door.

"Careful of cars," I yelled to her, and noticed Rachel and the Sid guy, still talking as if we hadn't even been there, as if I hadn't yelled at all.

Sid went into the army the next week, Special Forces, and the following June, the day after Rachel finished high school, he came for her. They got married in Myrtle Beach, no waiting period, and on the way back to Fort Bragg, Sid driving, they hit and killed an old woman crossing the highway. After that Sid asked not to be sent to Vietnam, said he wouldn't feel right killing someone, and the army complied. They made him a medic, and said he'd only have to go if the situation worsened.

Soon after that, Rachel had Mike, my first nephew. They bought a mobile home, cheap in those days. Sid never went to Vietnam, even wheeled an early discharge, and less than two years after my sister left she came home, kind of.

Home for my sister became Chesterville, not Aiken. Sid sold insurance. They bought a house with a VA loan, selling their trailer from North Carolina for a down payment. Rachel took care of the house and the kid, had a couple of more kids, twins, and when Sid got an offer from Nationwide Insurance down in Columbus, she left Knox County and Aiken forever.

The last time I was in Columbus, 1983, they still lived there, in a four-bedroom home on the north side. Two acres with a row of poplars on the west property line and an apple orchard in the back, a sheltered redwood deck with a gas grill. They'd had two more kids, twins again, and seemed very happy.

Since then I've written Rachel every few months or so, but it's not the same.

I miss her.

When Rachel left for North Carolina with Sid, Linda took over behind the counter. Her man was a truck driver from Newark, ran produce from there to restaurants out in the counties. We didn't sell diesel there at the store by then, not enough call for it—I think he just stopped by for a rest, or a soda. I was out pumping some gas the first time he came by.

He strutted up to me saying something or other, or at least working his mouth, but he'd left his truck running and the reefer on on his trailer, and I couldn't hear him.

"What?" I yelled, and with my free hand pointed towards his rig.

He turned around and looked at it, cocked his head as if puzzled, then came closer, smiled. teeth shiny like a Frigidaire, and yelled to me, "Can I park her there for a bit?"

"Sure," I said. I didn't care. He nodded toward the porch.

"Could a guy take a load off for a bit?" he said. He smelled ripe like the bottom of a basket of apples, sharp, acidic.

"Sure," I said. I didn't care what he did, just as long as he got that smell away from me. He went and plopped himself down in one of the rockers, splayed his legs out, and dropped his arms to his sides. Like the chair was his and always had been.

It was mid-summer 1974, sunny and hot, and my mother was inside taking a nap. My father was over at the Brackens', his in-laws, probably showing them how to replace the shear pin in their hay baler. Or something. I took my customer's money, gave her change, smiled when she did, then went inside. I gave the money to Linda behind the counter.

"Who's the guy out front?" she said. Her hands were quick, a blur, as she put the money in the register drawer.

"Don't know," I said. "Just wanted to sit a bit." A *bit* were his words, twice. Funny how I made them mine.

"I'll see if he needs anything," she said, and went outside. She had wide hips then, only a few inches on each side between the door jambs. Still has those hips as far as I know. She stayed outside quite a while talking to the truck driver, standing over him, eventually laughing, looking interested, using her hands from time to time, probably for unneeded emphasis—our father often talked that way. I watched her, and him, through the store's broad front window. I don't know what they said.

He made our place a regular stop after that, maybe twice a week, always sitting on the porch, always talking to my sister Linda, always for a long time taking her away from the register. Once in a while she'd get a bottle of Coke from the machine just inside. Sometimes she'd just take him out a glass of water. Once I was standing at the window watching, just idly watching, and Jane, twelve then, came up beside me.

"Who's the geek?" she said. I think she had most of her vocabulary fixed by the time she was eight or nine.

"Just some truck driver," I said. I noticed then she had grown some: I was a couple of inches short of six feet tall, and she came near to my shoulder.

"She's going next, isn't she?" said Jane.

"Suppose so," I grunted.

"What a shithead."

Within a few months, Linda and the trucker, Hap was his name, were married. The service was at the church on the road to Ankneytown, the church was still there then. Rachel still lived down in North Carolina, so Jane played maid of honor. She wasn't an ugly girl, though her ears were a little large and her nose a bit wide and she had these big ovate nostrils. But her in the dress made me laugh. I'd just never really seen her in one. Her new breasts bulged out of the low neckline, and she simply looked as uncomfortable as she must have felt.

"Laugh again," she said, "and I'll punch your lights out."

My sister Jane was growing up, acquiring her own personality, such as it was.

My father wore a suit that day, a skinny brown tie and a jacket with padded shoulders. He looked like Robert Mitchum in that movie from his and my mother's first date. Tall and broad and crooked. My mother, though, pretty as she was, only looked like herself, like my mother, not Jane Russell. I hadn't yet found that picture.

Hap had rented an apartment in Newark until then, but soon after Linda moved in with him they bought a house, a fifties ranch out by Moundbuilders Country Club. She got work as a receptionist in a dentist's office, and he became a city cop. They had two kids, one boy and one girl, about a year apart, and seemed a perfectly happy couple. The Christmas before Audrey and I left Aiken, though, Linda and Hap came over as always, and they told us Hap was working for Brinks or somebody, refilling twenties in all-night banking machines. He had beaten up some kid he was supposed to just be ticketing for a traffic violation or something, and he had been given a desk job while he saw the psychiatrist, who he eventually told to get fucked. It was working out for the best, though, Linda said. Hap was working longer hours now, on call half his time off, but at least she didn't have to worry so much and his new money was making the house payments easier.

I don't know, though. We write now and then, and in her last letter she told me they were separating. He'd been arrested for propositioning some undercover cop prostitute. With his experience he should have known better, you'd think.

I hope they work it all out, for the sake of my niece and my nephew if not for their own. From what I've heard, kids do better in a stable environment.

After Linda left, Jane didn't take over behind the counter. She was too young, and the law by then said you had to be fourteen. My parents had her do housework while my mother worked out front and my father helped the Brackens with their farming. Even then, though, Jane didn't do what she was supposed to. She spent most of her time across the road or out in the woods with Stevie Lubbers's younger sister Christine, sixteen but already we knew she was going to be a dyke, how could you help but know?

Maybe that's what began to screw up the relationship between Jane and my father, Jane never doing what my parents needed her to do. And you couldn't talk to her, at least I couldn't. She'd always just say, "You're being a shithead," and that would be that, and she'd go off and do whatever she did with Christine.

When she got to be fourteen, she still wouldn't be where she was supposed to be, still wouldn't work behind the counter, so my mother had to, nothing anyone could do about it. And though we didn't know of the cancer then, we did in a couple of more years, and I think that's why my father on his deathbed told Jane, "You killed your mother," and so forth, and why he died hating her and why they especially in those last couple of years seemed to loathe each other and always fought and yelled and changed everything.

I don't know why she made that show at his funeral, seeing as how she hated him and he hated her and all. Maybe though, if I can give her the benefit of the doubt, she cried just because she wished things between them would have been different.

I don't know.

When she was eighteen, in 1980, Jane moved to Columbus with Christine, into the upstairs of a house up on Neil Avenue. They had a dog, a firehouse dalmatian named Sappho, and Jane was studying poetry at Ohio State. Not reading, or analyzing, or criticizing, but writing. Jane was studying to be a poet.

I guess there's got to be one in every family.

Maybe *she* should be keeping the journals.

I made this entry today, thinking not of my sisters, but of Nati, the young woman without a family who works for me over at Daddy Rabbit's and here at my Tela house. It's a poem, I guess. At least I'll call it that. Some people might read it and call it obscene. I'd rather think of it as playful.

July 12, 1992

She lies on her back in the clear bathwater,
Draws her knees up towards her shoulders
To show me the ghost hair on her feet and toes
Barely there. She lies on her back in the clear

Bathwater, waits for me to tell her I want
To touch it, to bite it, to tickle it,

To shave it. And she knows I can't.
I have inherited this panda shyness
From my mother or my old best friend Steve

And she knows it, so she lies
On her back in the clear bathwater, teasing,
Leaving me wondering if she teases mocking,

Cruel, because she knows I want to touch it,
To bite it, to tickle it, to shave it,
And she knows I want to tell her.
Or is she just being playful, lying
On her back in the bathwater, me
On the passionless toilet surrounded

By perishing candlelight,
Or is this some sort of revenge for last night
When because of the Cuervo

I couldn't get it up and on her back,
With me lying naked in waiting,
She had to do herself.

Jerry Hopkins

No Gerard Manley Hopkins, I guess. Not even, again I guess, a Jane Hopkins.

But I didn't ask for this name, and I didn't ask for this job.

CHAPTER V
HERMIE AND THE OTHERS

For as long as I can remember, and presumably longer, my father spent more time with the Brackens, his in-laws, than with us at home. As I said, they moved up from Cincinnati in 1951, into Harry and Thelma Melvin's place. Down in Cincinnati, my grandfather-to-be Herman Bracken had worked for twenty-some years at Proctor and Gamble, most of the time in management. But he had grown tired of it somehow, nine-to-five and dealing with numbers and people here and there but never having anything to show for his life but a newer toothpaste and a house close to the suburbs but not quite there—who would really want to live like that? close but not quite—and couldn't he use his *hands* for something finally, get dirt under his fingernails, maybe some calluses on his fingers, maybe live off the land and on what he himself could produce.

Trouble was, Herman Bracken's aptitude was for numbers, not for machines. Without my father's constant help, he could produce nothing. My maternal grandfather was, in some sense, a poet, not a mechanic:

With his sons, he wanted to hunt the meat his family would eat. You've heard how that turned out. Now two feet, now one!

He wanted to grow and harvest their fruit, apples and cherries and pears from Harry Melvin's near-primordial orchard. All his trees could bear, though—despite his background in chemicals, he had no sense of pest control—was worm-infested and inedible.

He wanted to farm their vegetables and their grains, but he had no idea how the farming machinery he had taken over from Harry Melvin really worked, or why, which was inexplicably always his primary concern. And without my father's help, from the time a few weeks after my father met my mother until the day he died, I'm sure Herman's whole family would have starved. My mother would have died before she got the chance to marry my father, and I never would have been born. What a tragedy that would have been.

My first memory of Grandpa Herman dates to sometime around 1956 or 1957. (Some people say they can remember back to when they were only two years old. I can't, and I don't believe those who say they can. They're pulling some head trip.) He used to drive his two-tone Chevy Bel-Air over, though the walk was less than a mile or so, and you'd think if he was going to do country life he'd want to walk instead of drive. Stay closer to the earth. He would come in through the store's front door sporting his perpetual village-idiot smile, he'd let the screen slam behind him, and he'd yell out in a voice piercing like an old sewing machine, "Where's that son-in-law of mine?" I'd usually be the first person he'd see, sitting maybe cross-legged on the wooden floor in front of the counter, and he'd direct his words at me. I'd flinch, and then he'd go on into the back room, into our house, without another word. He'd leave the single but varied odor of cherry-blend pipe tobacco and pig manure—his next-door neighbors the Shermans raised pigs—behind him.

Within a few minutes, he and my father would be heading back out the front door, my father usually carrying his gray Craftsman tool box and explaining something with both his voice and his free hand, making it sound like whatever he was saying was something anybody would already know, and why was my grandfather bothering him about something so simple. But he'd always go anyway. My father was a good man.

This routine played out almost daily up until the time my father got sick with the cancer. In the year following, my grandmother Elizabeth, Herman's wife, got sick too, cancer, then died herself. My grandfather, then in his late seventies and saying he couldn't make the farm work anymore, and saying rightly but what was the news, took her down to Cincinnati to bury her and never came back.

He died two years later, December of 1983, when Audrey and I were living in Denver. Heart attack, not cancer like the rest of the family.

You couldn't blame the Pleasant Hill Lake Nuclear Weapons facility for *that* now, could you?

Audrey and I came back from Colorado for Grandpa Herman's funeral. We took a train, the first time for both of us, and we agreed later that it seemed like everyone was always staring at us. Silence, vacant, but for the steady rhythmic rumbling of steel wheels on uneven tracks.

We'd never been to Cincinnati. Grandpa was buried in a Woodlawn Cemetery in the north side. It seems that every city has a Woodlawn. After the service and before the burial, I couldn't get Audrey up off the strange church's pew. She just sat there, wouldn't move, crying I suppose, no, I know. It broke your heart.

My maternal Grandma Elizabeth was seventy-one when she died, but as long as I knew her she never seemed older, or younger, than fifty or so. My concept of what being fifty years old meant changed over the years, of course, from an age incredibly old to, like now, something not so far away.

My forever perception of Grandma Elizabeth can be summed up pretty simply. She smelled like breakfast, looked like a gas stove in a dress (part of that might be because of how she smelled), worked crossword puzzles in ink and quickly, and spent a good deal of her time begging her husband, my grandfather Herman, to take her and her daughter June, my mother, and her sons, the two that hadn't yet moved down to Mount Vernon, back to Cincinnati and civilization.

In dying, she finally got at least half her wish.

The others. My grandfather Tom, my father's father, died on November 22, 1963, the same day as President Kennedy, so he only had to put up with my other grandfather's ignorance of how to live in Aiken for twelve years.

Lucky guy, my father must have thought more than once, though as I said he always helped Grandpa Herman when asked.

My paternal grandfather left the following in his journal:

June 12, 1961
I don't know how young Tom does it. Hermie is a moron. He's

going to kill somebody. He should go back home, where he will be in his element, and quit trying to be something he's not and never will be. We each have a niche in this world. Some are born to it and some grow into it.

Hermie's is definitely NOT here in Aiken.

Young Tom must have the patience of Job. I always knew he'd turn out to be a good boy.

Thomas Nelson Hopkins II

Needless to say, my grandfathers never got along all that well.

My paternal grandparents, Tom and the Dorothy that had had such a hard time delivering my father, lived with us in the back of the store, in the back of Hopkins General Merchandise. When I was born, we had four rooms back there: a kitchen and three bedrooms. Our toilet was outside, not an outhouse, but hooked on with plumbing and all, and a shower, but you had to go through the kitchen door then take a few steps left to get to it. That room out there always had a smell to it. A lot of years later, when I finally left Aiken, I would recognize it in gas station restrooms.

Believe it or not, I always felt comforted by the scent of gas station restrooms. It made me feel at home while I was on the road. Audrey never understood that—I'm not sure I do either—and with some things there's just no explaining.

Sometime around 1960, when my two grandparents and my parents and me and my first two sisters were stuffed into those four rooms with the toilet outside, my father added two more rooms and brought the toilet inside.

Aiken hadn't begun to die yet. The store must have still been doing well. Maybe my father still thought it all would have a future.

So then we had the kitchen, four bedrooms, and a central room with the upright Phillips radio in it—no television—that you might call a living room. My parents and grandparents still had their own bedrooms, but my sisters, Rachel and Linda, moved into one of the new rooms. I got my own.

When I finally learned to masturbate, that privacy sure came in

46

handy. I wonder if my father had foreseen that need, and that's why he built the additions.

"I'll wash the sheets, Mother!"

My grandfather Tom and my grandmother Dorothy weren't hard folks to get along with. I suppose you could say I loved them both. Like my father, Grandpa Tom was big like a bull and, despite his poetic tendencies, he was proficient with his hands. I guess that's where my father learned most of what he knew, who he inherited his mechanical instincts from.

Grandpa Tom's poetic tendencies. He never spoke much, but when he did his voice boomed, almost made you want to duck:

"YOU JUST CAN'T STAND PROSPERITY, CAN YOU?" I remember him saying to me once, right after I had blown a third-grade spelling test.

And, "YOU HAVE TO HAVE THE COURAGE OF YOUR CONVICTIONS," to my father, once when my father, usually alert to such things, had let his guard down and allowed himself without complaining to be overcharged for some canned chili or something.

Grandma Dorothy didn't speak much either, but with her teeth in a glass on the table beside her she knitted a lot, darned all our socks when they got holes in them. She hardly ever put her teeth in, I guess they pained her somewhat, and when she did talk we usually couldn't understand her.

"Mlump," she would say, looking up through her knitting or darning and through the top halves of her bifocals, then, "Mlump mlump mlump." If she was scolding one of us, we could usually tell from her tone, emphatically high-pitched, but more often than not she was just in her own way making conversation.

"Put your teeth in, Mother," my mother June—she called both Dorothy and Elizabeth Mother—would have to say, always gently. And sometimes Grandma Dorothy would take the teeth from her glass, one plate at a time, shake the water from them, and then put them in and fix them in place with her tongue.

"June," she might say then, "I need more yarn," maybe repeating maybe not, what she had said toothless. We never knew.

Grandma Dorothy outlived Grandpa Tom, but not by much. As I said, Grandpa died in November of 1963, the same day as Kennedy. Heart attack. Grandma had her heart attack, then died, on the following Christmas Eve. I've always wondered if maybe it was a sign of Christmas charity that the God I still believed in at the time made us this gift, made sure there were enough heart attacks to go around.

So neither my parents nor half my grandparents lived to ripe old ages. This bothers me. I wonder what I might have passed along to my son Moses back in Arizona.

I've made a list of my parents and grandparents, how old they were when they died, and how they died:

Grandpa Herman Bracken, 73, heart attack,

Grandma Elizabeth Bracken, 71, cancer,

Grandpa Tom Hopkins, 65, heart attack,

Grandma Dorothy Hopkins, 71, heart attack,

Tom Hopkins, my father, 57, cancer,

June Hopkins, my mother, 49, cancer.

The cancer we can blame on the weapons plant, I suppose, but what about the heart stuff? Bad genes?

Maybe I should find some way to warn Moses.

I'm near forty now, and looking at this list I have to assume that I have fewer years ahead of me than I do behind, fewer years of what-nexts than I have years of memories.

This is the first time I've noticed this.

It's a bit depressing.

I've taken up smoking here in Tela, as far as I know the first one in my family to do so, except for Jane, of course. That was another thing that as a child she was always getting in trouble for, her and her friend Christine, Stevie's little sister. I smoke Guatemalan cigarettes, Rubios, from the Spanish word for blond, Gonzalo, the still-missing Gonzalo, has told me. They're menthols, and pretty good, I suppose, though I don't really have anything to compare them with, never having smoked back in the states, not once.

I've taken up smoking. I hear back there people are stopping, it's bad for you. But considering my recent family history, what have I got to lose?

I've just looked up the word *rubio* in my Spanish/English dictionary, just to make sure that what I told you from hearsay about it is correct. It is, but I also found an interesting entry for a *tabaco rubio*. It means Virginia tobacco. My ancestor George Wythe Hopkins originally came from Virginia, and you'll recall that until me almost all the men in my family were named after famous Virginians. It may be a sign that I may be neither a poet nor a mechanic that I can't decide if there is some web-like connection at work here or if it's just another of life's meaningless coincidences.

Moses. In 1967, my father bought a Ford pick-up, a turquoise F-100, from Jimmy Bracken, his nephew down in Mount Vernon. It became mine when he died, and it's the same truck that took Audrey and me from Aiken to Granville, then to Columbus, then Denver, then Wyoming's Flying Z, and finally to Tucson. I traded it in there, to a man whose ad in the *Daily Star* read as follows:

Buick—'76 LeSabre, very good condition. $550 or
trade for boat, pick-up, motorcycle, or shotgun.
325-etc.

When he drove it away from our house, the chrome "Bracken's Quality Ford" still shone intact from its tailgate. I've always wondered if he eventually traded our old truck for a shotgun.

I left the LeSabre with Audrey and little Moses. I probably left the boy with those bad genes swimming around inside his cells, too.

I wish I were more like my father.

CHAPTER VI
STEVIE KNEW, HE ALWAYS KNEW

Audrey and I never had any dates before we were married, not like my mother and father had. Her family's place was across the highway from ours and about half a mile south, two places down from the Lubbers's. We were the same age, and went to school and to church together. When we were finally married, in 1979, it seemed as if it were something arranged and we were simply concluding the arrangement late.

When Stevie Lubbers and I were kids, adolescents really (we had already begun to masturbate), we used to talk about who we were going to marry when we grew up. When we tired of playing army games back by the old canal—and as we grew older we tired of them more quickly, often wouldn't start them at all—we'd sometimes climb down into the ditch when it hadn't been raining and just walk, toss rocks, and talk. If it were summer the life-in-death aroma of freshly cut hay might accompany us.

"Sharon Johnson's not too bad," Stevie might say, looking up to me. He was a few inches shorter, though soon enough he'd shoot past six feet and stay there forever. I'd stay about the five-nine, five-ten I was then, stay there forever, and next to Stevie I'd always feel like a short man. I still do, and I don't even know him anymore.

If the sun was out he might be squinting. "And she's getting some tits," he might say.

"That's all you think about." Stevie was always talking about girls' breasts.

"I'll probably marry her, I think," he might say, so matter-of-factly, and he'd go up on his tiptoes, lean forward to glance past me up to the Johnson house, the first one south of his as we walked through the canal ditch.

"I don't know who I'd want," I'd have to say, and eventually we'd get down to the Marsh place, Audrey's, just past the Johnsons'. Mimicking Stevie, I'd look over to see if maybe Audrey was outside, helping her mother hang the laundry, feeding the chickens if it was early enough in the day, or just sitting in the shade if it was hot and afternoon. Sometimes she'd be there, and I'd feel my heart beat faster, and I'd start to sweat hot or not, and I'd hope my buddy Stevie didn't notice. Sometimes she'd be there, and she'd look over at us and smile, such pretty teeth, shining straight even from a distance, and those dimpled cheeks, I couldn't see them but I could imagine, remembering from school or church, and I'd think it was a hopeless thing, me and her: she had everything, she was gorgeous and her father's farm was the best around, always new equipment, and I was just some dumpy kid a little too tall that would someday take over the family store, never make it out of town, never be anybody.

"She'd be good for you," Stevie might say, nodding up towards Audrey's house if she was outside or not. "No tits though."

"No." Not then. But eventually she grew some, and though they weren't big and round, the kind Stevie might like, I found myself loving them almost as much as I loved her, loved everything about her.

Audrey's place. Though the Marshes didn't know it until I told them, after Audrey and I were married, their family came to Aiken right after the Civil War. They didn't know it because, as with most families, I came to find out, their ancestors never kept any written records. And at some point people start forgetting, or ignoring, their pasts. The present and the future become more important. Of course, I knew when the Marshes came because one of my ancestors, Benjamin Harrison Hopkins, had written of their arrival in his portion of the journals. This is what he had to say about Audrey's family:

April 30th, 1866

More than forty years ago my father, leaving his personal trials across the river, brought his family into what was then little more than wilderness, constructed his house and founded his business, and, envisioning economic and spiritual prosperity for himself and for his descendants, persevered despite barriers that from time to time must have made his ultimate success appear highly improbable. Beyond the opportunity to engage in fair trade, my father desired to build a community of like-minded souls who would each work for the good of others, who would display loyalty to family and neighbors above blind loyalty to nation.

A fortnight past, a new family joined us here in Aiken, and I believe my father, God rest his soul, would be pleased. The man, one Aaron Marsh, has come to us from Tennessee with his family, a lovely wife and four healthy children, and two wagons of farming implements and household wares, has negotiated the purchase of eighty acres from our friends the Mortons, and has already built his cabin, tomorrow he raises the barn. He will farm, he says, and what he does not use to feed his family he plans to sell, transport by canal and river to the cities, Cleveland north, down to Portsmouth and the Ohio south.

This Mr. Aaron Marsh, like my father and myself, seems proud to call himself a Copperhead. We have discussed the war now just over, its uselessness and its wasteful folly. As the war disrupted our trade and took my first son, so it destroyed his farm in Tennessee and cost him his two eldest. He wonders that he has anything left with which to begin again.

God bless him, this new addition to our still-burgeoning community. We need more like him. May he make Aiken his home for a long while.

Benjamin Harrison Hopkins

Like his father, George Wythe Hopkins, my ancestor Benjamin was self-educated. With him, though, if I can pause a minute to critique his style, it seemed to have worked.

Audrey's parents left Aiken a little more than a year before we did.

Retired to Arizona, a trailer park in Phoenix. Of course like the rest of Aiken's families, they hadn't been able to sell their place, so who knew where they got the money to call it quits. Old Noah, though he didn't know diddly about where he'd come from, must have over the years been a frugal enough businessman to ensure that, when the time came, he'd know where he was going.

"How's your grandfather?" Stevie might say there in the ditch, the two of us walking side by side in that leisurely, time-wasting way kids do when in summer they have nothing to do and all the time in the world to do it.

"Which one?"

"The dumb one," and he'd likely laugh, his orange bangs flopping up and down on his forehead. "I saw him limping over at your place a couple of days ago."

"That. He tipped the swather over. Had the blades too high, I guess. He wouldn't say, but ten to one he fell right out of the seat."

"I wouldn't say either, if I'd done something so stupid."

"Audrey Marsh, you think?" I might say, covertly slapping a glance up in the direction of her family's house.

"She ain't got any tits yet, but it's a natural."

I think Stevie was wise beyond his years, but Audrey and I were probably thirteen then, and it would take another thirteen years for us to finally get married. As I said, we went to school together—in those days *all* of Aiken's youngsters went to school together, of course. And we went to the same church, Aiken's only church, and in those days everyone attended church religiously, except for my Grandpa Herman, who apparently while working for Proctor and Gamble had developed for himself some sort of agnosticism, based on who knew what. Maybe knowing how chemicals worked and all, he couldn't see putting his faith in anything non-chemical, in an ethereal being like our God professed himself to be.

Anyway, we saw a lot of each other, me and Audrey Marsh, and now and then she'd come into the store, for thread or some such, while I was working. We never talked much, though. Not at school or at church or in the store. Not even at Stevie's wedding, although that would have been a prime wooing time, seeing as how weddings are romantic by nature.

I think it was my fault we never talked. I haven't always been the extrovert, the gregarious fellow, my customers here at Tela's Daddy Rabbit's believe me to be.

In 1971 Stevie, Steve by then and a good three inches taller than me, at nineteen married his next-door neighbor Sharon Johnson. I was his best man, Audrey her maid of honor. I almost died when I saw Audrey in the dress, lavender and lacy, her waist-length hair not yet gray, but would that have mattered? How could I say anything to her, knowing I might blurt out something stupid and make myself appear an idiot? And there I was almost dwarfed by the man Steve beside me, or so I thought, and six or so years earlier he had known what he was going to do then gone ahead and done it, at least as far as Sharon Johnson was concerned, and all I knew of myself was that forever I'd be stuck working in my family's store, someday taking it over but never really being anything, anything special, and somebody like Audrey Marsh deserved something special and certainly she knew it.

We graduated from high school the spring before Stevie's wedding, me and Stevie and Audrey and half a dozen others. You'd think Audrey and I would have been closer, would have known each other better. But we weren't, and we didn't, and that's that. Later we talked about it, this aloofness from each other that seemed it would never end, and all we could come up with was that it was my fault, although at the time we talked we were in love and the notion of fault didn't carry any negative connotations, nothing did. I just wouldn't pay attention to her back then, and she couldn't make the first move, being a girl, then a woman and all.

During those thirteen years, from the time that Stevie Lubbers said, "It's a natural," to the time Audrey and I got married, it seemed like everyone I knew had something to say about the me and Audrey that to them, especially to my nearest sisters (I was older and should have beat them to the marriage punch), inexplicably hadn't become me and Audrey.

"Maybe you could use another lesson or two," Rachel said cryptically right before she got married.

"Just talk to her," Linda said when she and Hap got back from their honeymoon, just a night at the Sheraton in Columbus, a room with cheap caviar and cheaper champagne overlooking the tenth-floor pool, but it was more than I'd experienced or at that time could expect to experience. "Don't think about it, just *do* it!"

After Rachel and Linda were married and gone, I overheard the remnants of my family talking of it one night, my nothingness. Our house in the back of Hopkins General Merchandise had grown several years back but it was still small, close enough that secrets couldn't remain secrets for long.

"Maybe he's queer," my father said, and I couldn't see him, but I could imagine his hands waving punctuation. I couldn't believe he said that, although in retrospect I'd given him every reason to think it, me being in my twenties by then and never having been with a woman as far as he knew. And I *was* still a virgin, who knows why, I'd only dreamed.

"You're being too hard on him," my mother said, her voice, rare as it was, still soft like an angora sweater, how it must have been for my father and always was for me.

Jane said, "Maybe he is a queer. What's wrong with that?" She sounded lonely. I don't think she and Christine had yet found their common calling.

My grandfather Tom was gone by then, years upon years, but I swear, though I know it's impossible, that through the thin walls I heard him say this:

"TO EACH HIS OWN."

Maybe I just hoped. Maybe I just missed him.

Whatever, everyone talked, and none of their talking ever helped.

My friend Stevie Lubbers. The September after Stevie—Steve—married Sharon Johnson, he moved them both into Columbus. Smart like a paper cut as well as wise, he had graduated tops in our small class, no one else was even close, and he got a scholarship to attend Ohio State. He finished in three and a half years, not four, just like him, got perfect grades again, and moved Sharon and their three kids—who knows where they found the time for that?—up to Massachusetts. He got a fellowship to some Boston law school, a free ride. I'm sure he deserved it.

Stevie and I kept in touch for a bit while he was at Ohio State, wrote letters here and there. After the first year or so, though, the writing stopped and we only talked when he came home for holidays. Then when he went away to Boston, we stopped talking completely. He had his life, I had mine, and I never heard from him again, only knew of his doings when someone in his family brought me up to date. I never heard from him again, but I heard enough to stay jealous, to wonder if I would ever be able to be the man Stevie had become.

No, not exactly never.

I got a letter from him a few weeks ago. I have no idea how he found me here in Guatemala, the letter didn't say. In fact it didn't say anything of a personal nature. It seems Stevie's a partner in a law firm in Columbus—his name came third on the letterhead—and it's contemplating handling some class action suit against the federal government and the Pleasant Hill Lake Nuclear Weapons Facility. On behalf of the former residents of Aiken, Ohio, the letter said.

That includes me, of course.

And Audrey too, though not my son Moses. He came later. I wonder if Stevie found me through her.

Pleasant Hill Lake sits a lot closer to Loudonville than to Aiken. Twenty, twenty-five miles north of my old home town. As it left the lake, though, the water, the suit says, thus the waste from the weapons plant, ran south by Aiken. And whenever it rained, especially when it flooded, the old ditch of a canal filled with hot stuff. We suspected that, back in the seventies when so many of Aiken's people started getting cancer and dropping dead before what should have been their time. The canal gave Aiken life, and, it may be, the canal took that life away.

Poetic, isn't it? The way things work.

Or perhaps it's simply Biblical. Certainly more than a few of Aiken's former residents would prefer that as an explanation.

Back to me and Audrey. Church finally brought us together. Not outside prodding, not personal shame, not desperate wrangling. Just church.

Christmas of 1977, when Stevie and Sharon Lubbers already had three kids and at the rate they were going probably five or six, when Stevie had likely already graduated from law school and landed a junior partnership in the company in Columbus he would eventually run—just guessing, I have no way of knowing for sure—Christmas of 1977, the pastor of Aiken's church, Brother Jarvis, decided that *this* year he would replace the usual children's pageant with a cantata to be performed by the adult choir. I sang in that choir, baritone, and so did Audrey, alto. She had a lovely voice despite, or maybe because of, its low range, a lovely voice, just like everything else about her.

We began practice for the cantata three weeks before Christmas. Mondays and Tuesdays, on top of our regular Thursdays. Wednesdays, of course, we had prayer meeting, and we had regular services Sunday mornings, training union Sunday nights. That left only Fridays and Saturdays free for those three weeks.

Busy, but I didn't have a wife, or kids, and by then the store wasn't doing shit, and my father was still running it anyway. Nothing else to do.

More on the church. It had a choir loft at its rear. When you entered the church, the loft's floor was the ceiling above you. It had six sturdy wooden pews, oak, three on each side with an aisle down the center, and a railing, solid and maybe two and a half, three feet high kept you if you were clumsy from falling forward into somebody's lap on the ground floor and maybe breaking one of your bones or theirs or both. It was a solid railing, not columnar, you couldn't see through it, and on winter days when it was really too cold to be outside the loft made a good hiding place for kids.

When I was twelve or so, and my sister Rachel probably ten, Rachel taught me how to kiss up in that choir loft—maybe that was the lesson she would refer to years later—first just puckering and touching lips, like you might kiss your mother or your grandmother, your sister if somebody made you, then tongue. I never knew people did that. I don't know where Rachel learned to do it, either, and I felt a little embarrassed that she, younger than me, was the one doing the teaching. Still I couldn't wait to try it out on Audrey, knowing I never would really, how could that happen, but at least I could dream.

In 1977 up in the choir loft I stood between Audrey's father Noah—he sang bass—and my father Tom, like me a baritone. And a pretty damn good one. His cancer hadn't shown up yet. They were both better than me, with voices louder and more resonant. I usually couldn't hear myself over them, and I figured nobody else could either. Just as well. I didn't mind going through the motions. So when Brother Jarvis went down the list of solos matching names with parts I just assumed he'd pass me by.

It didn't turn out that way, not exactly. Like I'd hoped and figured, I didn't get chosen for a solo. I'd be doing a duet. With Audrey Marsh...

Oh, God.

Audrey normally stood the row behind me, her mother Naomi, another alto, on her right, my mother June, a soprano, on her left. But for our duet, Brother Jarvis moved us next to each other, me at the inside end of the baritones, her at the inside end of the altos.

"Better able to synchronize," Brother Jarvis said. He always spoke of the choir in mechanical terms. It was a machine, he said, whose parts needed to function together, whose gears need to mesh. Strange words, for a man whose rhyming sermons made you think he might be God's chosen poet.

For three weeks then, three nights a week, Audrey and I stood elbow to elbow. When she sang I could smell her breath, warm like fur-lined gloves and fragrant like honeysuckle. She didn't use perfume as far as I could tell, but naturally she didn't have to. I imagine she could smell my breath too. I discovered breath mints that December, wintergreen Certs.

"To-day He lives," Audrey sang, Mondays and Tuesdays and Thursdays for three weeks and then finally Christmas Eve, "bring-ing us Sal-va-tion. To-day He lives," she sang, and her voice next to me killed me, "All hope to give."

How could I follow that? Me!

"To-day I know," I sang after her, Mondays and Tuesdays and Thursdays for three weeks and then finally Christmas Eve, "He holds the fu-ture," and my voice the first night or two cracked and that killed me too, but then it smoothed out, and somehow we started walking to choir practice together then church Sundays and prayer meeting Wednesdays, "and life will be worth liv-ing," I finished, "be-cause to-day He lives."

"What would you like to do today?" Audrey said a week or so before the performance, finding me stripping and waxing a section of the store's floor. I always did it a piece at a time to leave room for customers to get around.

"Don't know," I said, looking at her then not, knowing if I kept look-ing it would turn to a stare. My folks brought me up not to be rude. "You free?"

"Till dinner."

"How about a walk?"

"I'll get my other shoes."

And so forth. Not much, I know, but we were, I guess, falling in love. We didn't need much.

We went for the walk, enjoyed it, and a couple of days later I found it surprisingly easy to just walk on down to her house, no courage required. I expected to find her out back with the chickens. They have a particular odor, a reek maybe like Limburger if you're not used to it. Turned out she was in the kitchen, boiling chicken bones and vegetable scraps for soup stock, filling the room with the aromas of dill weed and allspice and sage and such. I sat at the kitchen table, and Audrey stood stirring with her back to me, her graying hair pulled tightly and hanging in a ponytail halfway down her back.

"You reaching a stopping point?" I said, and I wanted to put my hands gently on her waist and kiss her bare, freckled neck just below her ear, but I didn't.

"You sound like you've got something in mind," she answered with a wink in her voice. "Do you?" she prodded.

"Nothing special," I answered. And I waited for her, just watched her practiced, perfect movements, and wondered if I could really be so lucky.

"To-day He lives," we sang together in harmony those blue-eyed nights, her voice higher than mine and in its cool raspiness lower, like a woman's voice is,

"Bring-ing us sal-va-tion," we sang,

"To-day the Sav-iour lives."

"HAL-LE-LU-JAH!" the choir in its entirety sang, twenty Grandpa Toms, but with melody in their voices, life like never, and Audrey and I, beneath them, again in harmony,

"Lord we praise Thee,"

"HAL-LE-LU-AH!"

"Lord we praise Thee," and now, following Brother Jarvis's directions more worshipful, Audrey and I now with the choir, Eileen Jarvis perfection on the piano, all of us together, together,

"HAL-LE-LU-JAH!" and there on Christmas Eve it didn't matter that so few filled the pews to listen, because for all of us everyone that mattered *was* there, and it didn't matter that my younger sisters had married first, or that Stevie Lubbers had always known, because now I knew too. Me and Audrey Marsh had finally found each other.

CHAPTER VII
THE DRAFT, GOING NOWHERE

My part-time next-door neighbor here in Tela—publicly Miguel Romero from Guatemala City—is really Michael Roberts from Chicago, Illinois. He grew up there, and being a couple of years older than me reached his teens in time to be a sixties hippie, smoking pot and wearing tie-dye and protesting the war and so forth. He says he later worked for the CIA, came down a few years before me to do some work for the Ríos Montt government, decided fuck it all and stayed, changing both his name and his business. I'm surprised they let him do it. Now he exports Indian-made fabrics and clothes back to the states, mostly to stores owned by his own spy-business buddies, he says. Mostly around D.C. and New York, but a couple in Los Angeles, even one in Tennessee, of all places. If I still ran Hopkins General Merchandise, I might be jealous of his connections.

This CIA stuff, not to mention Miguel's being a regular American and all, astonished me the first time I heard it. He's a little guy, even shorter than me though more stocky, like a tree stump with shorts, a t-shirt, and glasses. He looks more a plodder than a slitherer.

Oh well. The first time I heard it, I still believed things, and people, were what they appeared to be.

Guatemala. My new country.

This Efraín Ríos Montt isn't around anymore—who knows where old generals here in Guatemala disappear to?—but Miguel has told me some about him. He ran for president back in '74, as a Christian Democrat, whatever that is—in the states you're either Democrat or Republican, or like my family nothing. He won, but the army didn't like it. They wanted somebody else to be their president, a different general, Laugerud García. Ríos Montt, probably saying something like, "Fuck them, then," though in Spanish of course, en español—where's Gonzalo?—lit out for Spain. Who knows why, except that maybe they speak the same language.

He came back in 1977, ran for president again in '78, and this time lost outright.

SOME PEOPLE JUST CAN'T TAKE NO FOR AN ANSWER.

He renounced Catholicism, maybe figuring his losing was their fault, not his (from what Miguel says, you need the backing of the Catholics almost as much as you need the army if you're going to be president). He joined a protestant church that called itself the Word church, a branch of these Gospel Outreach people from somewhere back in northern California. The California people must have had some CIA connections. It was after Ríos Montt hooked up with them that Miguel Romero, still Michael Roberts then, showed up.

In 1982, it seems some other generals, maybe some new ones, didn't like the way their president at the time, still another general, a Lucas García, was running the war against the guerrillas. They did a coup, tossed him out, said they wanted this Ríos Montt fellow instead.

You following?

Miguel tells me that Ríos Montt was running a day school for his church in Guatemala City then, and that at the precise instant he got the call he was busy cleaning the school's toilets. You've got to wonder how Miguel knows that.

Sometime in 1983, just before Miguel Romero changed his name and his business, some more generals got pissed at his buddy Efraín and tossed him out. I guess his new God couldn't help him, not surprising, and this General Mejía Victores took over. He was gone by the time I got here in 1985, though. The country had held some elections, and this civilian, Vinicio Cerezo, had been chosen president. The army for some reason had allowed him to stay.

He's gone now too, though, replaced by another civilian in another election, but I don't know who. It's hard to keep track, and I've got a business to run. The new guy likely won't be around long anyway.

An aside to *los generales*:

Hey, guys, there's a little town up in central Ohio ready for somebody to come in and take it over. It's going cheap!

The sixties.

Like the Depression of the thirties, the unrest of the sixties, the time of Miguel Romero's impetuous youth, passed us by in Aiken.

This I know. I was there.

We knew about Vietnam. It was in the newspapers, of course. On the radio Paul Harvey mentioned it almost every day, and on television Walter Cronkite gave us the pictures and his commentary. And you'll remember my brother-in-law Sid came through town on his way to volunteer, though again that was in '71, but in memory the sixties and the early seventies kind of run together to all be a piece of the same time, you know how it works.

You'd think my father would have had something to say about the whole deal, having himself attended one war. But his critique could legitimately be reduced to the following:

"Same old shit."

So much for patriotism and the Hopkins family.

In the papers and on radio and on TV we heard about the riots too, in Watts, in Detroit. All cities, all folks of color, mostly. But Aiken wasn't a city, far from it, and we were all white, from Virginia and Tennessee and before that Europe I suppose, England or Ireland or somewhere like that. The world of riots and race problems was as far removed from us as sweet potato pie is from cactus jelly, if you know what that is.

We heard about the drugs too, how could you not, but as far as I know none of Aiken's people had anything to do with them. Aiken didn't exactly sit on any main drag, and we were all farmers and such. My father drank coffee most mornings, bourbon too, most of the time. And now and then Grandma Elizabeth and Grandpa Herman took a bottle of brandy, Christian Brothers, down from behind the crystal on their kitchen cupboard's top shelf, usually around Christmas, and poured everybody, we kids included, drinks in these tiny glasses about the size of your thumb, little more than a sip. But, at least in my family, nobody ever smoked, not even Jane, she was too young at the time. Marijuana would have choked us all. And we kept some aspirin around the house, but a bottle of a hundred or so usually lasted a year or more. My mother June always said it was best to let the sickness just run its course. When the news people would talk about reds and whites and yellows, then, it meant nothing to us.

The sixties was just another decade for us back there in Aiken.

We're in the nineties now, and Aiken is dead, and the nineties might not end up being anything special by the time they're over, though it being the end of the millennium and all you could hardly expect them not to be in some way spectacular.

If Aiken was still the way it was in the sixties, though, and still alive (as much as a place like Aiken could be), what would it matter even if the world ended? We wouldn't notice.

As for me in the sixties, I learned how to masturbate and to kiss, remained a virgin, developed a deathless though apparently hopeless love for Audrey Marsh, and began my career as a church-choir baritone.

Generals, wars, armies.

The Hopkins family has almost always sent its boys to war, and almost always done it grudgingly. Benjamin Harrison Hopkins, you'll remember, didn't go into the War Between the States though he was only thirty-five or thirty-six when it started, instead stayed in Aiken and bitched about it. His son went though, Richard Henry Lee Hopkins, and died at eighteen after, not in, the Battle of Chattanooga, swimming, typhoid. My grandfather's uncle and namesake, the first Thomas Nelson Hopkins, bit it in the Spanish-American War. My grandfather never knew him, was born ten days before he died. Then my grandfather Tom Nelson II, he had World War I, which he survived, of course, minus that one arm, but then you've heard in the journal what *he* thought about the war. And my father went to the Pacific in World War II, and he was ready to go, wanted to. He came out alive and with all his parts, but who knows what happened to his insides. He never talked about the war. And when Korea came around he was still of age, but he didn't have to go because among other things, he was his father's only son, though he could have gone anyway. Either he thought he'd seen enough or else somebody, my bitter-at-the-government grandfather for instance, talked him out of it. Whatever, my father sat that one out.

Noah Marsh's brother Abe fell on his face on the beach at Inchon and didn't get up—he had no parts from the waist down. But he didn't become a part of my family, or me a part of his, depending upon how you look at it, until almost thirty years after he died.

I guess he doesn't count, Audrey's would-be Uncle Abe.

My war would have been Vietnam. They still had the draft then, and I figured that as soon as I turned eighteen in November, I'd be out of high school, they'd tab me and I'd be going, no questions asked, of course. I always did what I was told. Near the end of our senior year Stevie and I talked about it a lot. He would turn eighteen in May and be eligible, but he wouldn't get drafted, he was sure, and even if he did he'd be able to get a student deferment. He'd already been accepted at Ohio State. I wasn't going to college though, my grades not being all that good and of course I was old enough now to start learning the money end of the family business. My folks expected it and so did I. I had to worry.

One day in April Stevie Lubbers and I were sitting in the new spring grass underneath the willows back behind his house, facing the ditch and throwing rocks across it, over to where the Germans used to hide.

"It's not like they pick everybody," Stevie said. Easy for him to say. "You're probably worrying for nothing." He had grown by then, but his voice hadn't grown with him. It was still high-pitched and squeaky like a dry thumb on clean porcelain. "Enjoy the day."

"That's easy for you to say," I said, and there might have been some bitterness in my voice. I couldn't help but feel jealous of my old friend, just a little bit, just a little jealous, an emotion I didn't welcome.

Stevie was confident, sure, but he still checked the mail every day as soon as my Aunt Jill Bracken from down in Mount Vernon drove off after stuffing it in the Lubbers's box at the road. Every day, I'd see him through the front window of Hopkins General Merchandise. He never got his notice though, and in the fall he went off to Ohio State without it.

In time the government announced that their method for drafting kids was changing, they were going to a lottery based on your birthday.

Stevie was home from college when the numbers were due to be announced, and at four o'clock in the morning, still dark, still night, of the day they'd be listed in the paper we sat in the rockers on the porch of my family's store, waiting for my cousin Hank Bracken from down in Mount Vernon—my Uncle Fred, who by then owned the newspaper, was making him start at the bottom, the only way to really get a feel for the business—waiting for my cousin Hank to drop off his morning bundle. I was nervous—who wouldn't be with his future at stake?—and though he didn't show it so much Stevie must have been too. Student deferments had been done away with. Everybody called had to go, and though this was 1970, almost 1971, and Stevie didn't have his wife Sharon Johnson to worry about yet, he knew he would have soon. Stevie always knew what he wanted.

"Have you talked to your father about it?" Stevie asked me.

"He won't talk," I said.

"War's hell."

"Must be. All he ever says is 'same old shit.'"

"McGill up in Montreal has a good pre-law," he said. "Cigarette?" He held out his pack to me, must have picked it up at college, and when I shook my head, with his teeth he took a cigarette into his mouth, then he pulled off his gloves, took the matches out from the pack's cellophane wrapper, and lit it. He tossed the match into the snow, it hissed, and as he puffed on the cigarette the tip glowed and lit up his face.

My friend Stevie, is all I could think.

He said, "Canada's got a different kind of justice, though."

"You'll pick it up," I said. Of course I hoped he wouldn't have to. "You afraid?"

"You?"

And so forth to nothing.

After awhile I noticed it was getting lighter, not yet sunrise, far from it, but just light enough, especially with the snow, that you could begin to make out more than outlines. It looked peaceful like a Norman Rockwell. My cousin Hank hadn't shown yet, and without announcing it I went inside for my father's bourbon. He always kept a bottle behind the vinegar, same size and shape. It was half full, and by the time the papers came, me and Stevie had finished it off.

On the list we found Stevie's number first, his was more important. He had drawn three hundred forty-five. He'd be going back to Columbus, be allowed to marry Sharon Johnson and have a bunch of kids and then go on to his Boston law school and then practically head his own firm.

I'd been given three hundred thirty-three.

I wouldn't be going anywhere.

I leaned over the front railing and threw up into the virgin snow. I couldn't see colors, just a black blemish, still too dark. All I'd drunk until that time in my life was brandy, and just a bit of that, and the whiskey didn't set well in my stomach.

I wouldn't be going anywhere.

CHAPTER VIII
TOO WET TO PLOW

Audrey and I COURTED—that's what my grandfather Tom would have called it if he had still been around—for more than a year before we finally married. We did that January 7, 1979, at Aiken's church, the last wedding to be held at the place, probably forever. Brother Jarvis presided: he'd be in town a few more months. My father stood up for me—his cancer came two years later, and Stevie Lubbers was probably in Columbus, I didn't know then.

OUT OF SIGHT, OUT OF MIND, my grandfather Tom might have said.

Stevie's family had moved away just before last Thanksgiving, to Florida, retiring, they said. His sister Christine lived in their house by herself, would for another year and a half or so, when Jane graduated from high school and the two moved to Columbus. But Stevie and Christine didn't keep in touch. Sharon Johnson was of course with Stevie—Steve, damn it—so Audrey's mother Naomi served as her one and only attendant, not a bridesmaid, just someone to stand beside her, I guess.

All my sisters came. Rachel and Linda brought their husbands and what kids they had, five between them at the time, Rachel's second set of twins hadn't shown up yet. Jane, sixteen then, almost seventeen, naturally came with Christine. Jane wore blue jeans rather than a dress. I guess she'd had her fill of my mocking. The two held hands through most of the ceremony, and my still-Robert Mitchum father, whenever he looked their way, shot them a crooked frown of disapproval. He didn't say anything about them though, at least not during the ceremony. He had enough of a sense of propriety to save his scolding for later.

He was a wise man.

My grandfather Herman and my grandmother Elizabeth, in their seventies then, came. My father had to go pick them up. Herman didn't drive anymore, and Elizabeth never did so naturally she didn't now, special day or not.

My mother couldn't exactly make it, being dead and all, but she was buried right outside, and I think in some way maybe supernatural, maybe natural as could be, we all felt her presence, those of us who had loved her, I suppose all of us.

My mother.

As I said, when she died in the summer of 1978, it was a quick process. Three months beginning to end—if you don't count the near fifty years she lived before—the last two weeks in Knox County Hospital down in Mount Vernon. Those last weeks my father spent every second with her there, from intensive care to the cancer ward, then back to intensive care then out. I watched the store. Jane helped.

The Sundays of those two weeks I closed the store down and skipped church, took Jane and the pick-up to the hospital. The first Sunday, my mother was in her own room on the fourth floor, but when we got there visiting hours hadn't yet begun. I usually had no trouble keeping such things straight, but not this time. We found my father in the waiting room, sleeping on a couch. The television above his head shouted a Sunday-morning preacher's pleas for money, and I turned the sound down and let the picture go. My father knuckled his eyes open, maybe he hadn't been asleep after all, and sat up.

"She's bad," he said, and he leaned forward resting his forearms on his knees. "We need to pray for her."

"It hasn't done any good so far," Jane said.

My father turned just his eyes toward me. "Why'd you bring her?" he said. Jane shuffled out of the room, and I didn't see her for a couple of more hours.

"I'll get us some coffee," I said. No use answering his question about Jane.

"No. Sit with me." I did. He took my left hand in his right, hot and a bit sweaty. "Let's pray."

He smelled ripe like a men's locker room. I bowed my head and closed my eyes, and he began:

"Dear Lord," he said. He rarely prayed, but when he did he always began as though he were dictating a letter. "Our dear wife and mother, June Hopkins, walks through the valley of the shadow of death today. Be with her, and if it is Thy will, take her from us. But remember, if You will, she is still young and until now full of life, of course You know that, I'm not saying You're making a mistake, You know me better than that, I've always tried to do right, look at the kids, I suppose You've even got a reason for Jane being the way she is…

"In Jesus name. Amen."

"Amen," I said.

"Bourbon?" He pulled his flask from his hip pocket.

"Can't dance," I said. TOO WET TO PLOW, my father's father Tom would certainly have finished.

The second Sunday, my mother's last, she had been moved back into intensive care. You couldn't visit her there, you had to stand outside the room and watch through a window. We did that. Jane was with us, with me and my father, but she hadn't said anything when we arrived and was silent now. I'd warned her. "I'll punch your lights out," I'd said during the drive down.

For the hours we stood there and watched, my mother never opened her eyes. We could see that much through the window and the tubes in her mouth taped to her face and the yellow mask like my father would be forced to wear three years down the road. She didn't sleep peacefully though. Now and then her body tensed and straightened, she looked like if she had the energy she would have screamed, and she'd roll a bit to one side or the other, then curl up fetal-like, then straighten again. The machines monitoring her didn't change much, she was staying pretty steady. But still the nurses would hear the commotion and run in. More often than not she was simply shitting herself and they'd have to change her gown and her sheets, but the tubes stayed where they were. They had become a part of her, I guess. Like new arms, legs. Tongues. Breasts.

It made me sad and somehow lonely. But most of all it made me angry, and it shook my faith. How could He? I must have cried from the shallows of my naivete.

My mother died that night, or rather the following morning long before dawn. My father's phone call woke me from a restless sleep in our house back of Hopkins General Merchandise. He made a journal entry, probably that Monday night when he asked me and Jane to leave him in peace and he went into his room, closed the door, and didn't come out for the night:

June 7, 1978

June died today.

T.J.H.

That was all, and as far as I can tell that's the last thing he wrote in the journal until Veteran's Day, sometime in November. Veteran's Day always seemed to liven him up. I don't know why.

Bracken's One-Stop Funeral Home—of another of my cousins on my mother's side of the family—handled the funeral. They held a day of open viewing down at their Monticello-like mansion-type place in Mount Vernon. My father had to choose a dress appropriate for the occasion, though what's really appropriate for a dead person to be seen in?— being dead and all, she couldn't possibly care. During the time of my mother's illness, Rachel and Linda had been around from time to time during the week to watch her and sit with our father, and they were around now of course. All three of my sisters, then, helped my father pick a dress, and they came up with one I'd only seen once, when as boys me and Stevie had been going through my parents' closet—just being curious boys, I guess—a four-by-eight back of their bedroom. I remember wondering why they'd need something so big. She only ever wore the same half-dozen or so dresses, plus one for Sunday, and Christ that closet took up damn near as much space as my whole room, it was half as big as one of the store's aisles. It was a slinky thing, the dress they chose, and black, and finally dead she looked the Jane Russell alluring, if I can say that of my mother, that though I couldn't think it at the time I can sure think now, having recently found that picture.

Everybody came to see her dead. At least everybody who loved her. I guess everybody.

Naturally my mother was buried in Aiken's cemetery, and she was the next to the last to be so. Bracken's dug the grave with a Ford backhoe, a 1500, then parked it out of sight behind the church until the funeral was over. Brother Jarvis said words, and for the rest of us, life went on, though not like before. But we managed, people always do.

"You may kiss the bride," Brother Jarvis said after Audrey and I did the whole normal vow thing, Do you Gerard Hopkins? Do you Audrey Marsh? (I don't remember the order, I must have been nervous) and so forth. Nothing not traditional. I lifted Audrey's veil and we kissed. She was wearing a strawberry lipstick, and I hadn't tasted it before, she never wore lipstick, or even make-up till then. She didn't have to. I didn't like the taste, and on top of that it made my mouth feel greasy. When my father and Audrey's father and the others shook my hand, with my free fingers I kept wiping away the crimson I knew must still be on my lips.

Despite my perfectly fitting rented tux (from Bracken's Formal Wear of Mount Vernon, still another cousin), I didn't feel so manly with the lipstick and all. If it's not too much of a cliché, I think I suddenly felt I was selling myself out cheap, trading my independence, my manhood, for a steady lay. What's new?

We walked back down the aisle and outside accompanied by Eileen Jarvis's dissonant piano. She had come down with a crippling arthritis, and her crooked fingers didn't always go where she wanted them to. Too bad. I remembered her years before playing pretty good, even for the Cantata in '77. During the ceremony, it had begun to sleet, and Audrey and I ran to my father's pick-up—he drove Herman and Elizabeth in their old Bel-Air—and led the chilled, wet procession to the reception at the Marsh place.

But back to death. My father's, May of '81, was not unlike my mother's. The cancer struck the same way, the only difference being that it took longer to kill him. Maybe he was stronger. I did the sitting and waiting at Knox County Hospital. Audrey watched the store by herself. Not much to do by then though, not much at all, and she knew the ropes.

I buried him myself. Next to my mother, naturally. His is so far the cemetery's final grave. We didn't have an open viewing like we had with my mother. By that time everybody was gone except for me and Audrey and his in-laws, and presumably most of them saw him in the refrigerator while my cousin treated him with the chemicals.

Of course Bracken's One-Stop provided the coffin and the embalming and the headstone at a reduced price, cost, us being family.

The soft spring ground made for easy digging, and that was good. I'd never been too good with a shovel.

Brother Jarvis was long gone. I spoke over the grave. Audrey stood beside me and cried. Grandpa Herman and Grandma Elizabeth, by that time Aiken's only other residents, stood with us. And of course Rachel, Linda, Jane, and the rest of their families came too.

My father had always had a love of poetry—my name hadn't just come out of the blue—so at his funeral I thought it appropriate to read some. I chose this, from Tennyson. It was one of his favorites, and though I didn't think of it at the time, I've since entered it in the journals. Some words simply must be preserved.

Here it is:

> *I cannot rest from travel; I will drink*
> *life to the lees. All times I have enjoyed*
> *Greatly, have suffered greatly, both with those*
> *That loved me, and alone; on shore, and when*
> *Through scudding drifts the rainy Hyades*
> *Vexed the dim sea. I am become a name;*
> *For always roaming with a hungry heart*
> *Much have I seen and known—cities of men*
> *And manners, climates, councils, governments,*
> *Myself not least, but honored of them all—*
> *And drunk delight of battle with my peers,*
> *Far on the ringing plains of windy Troy,*
> *I am a part of all that I have met;*
> *Yet all experience is an arch Wherethrough*
> *Gleams that untraveled world whose margin fades*
> *Forever and ever when I move.*
> *How dull it is to pause, to make an end,*

To rust unburnished, not to shine in use!
As though to breathe were life!

I'm thinking now that my father left me without ever telling me of his war, of his sights in the Pacific he must have seen, the bonds with his fellow warriors he must have felt. I always figured he'd eventually get around to it, but he never told me. Never mentioned it in his section of the journals either.

I was going to describe for you here me and Audrey's wedding reception, but the hell with it. Nothing important happened.

The church. "The church." Site of weddings, lessons, cantatas, funerals and burials. As Audrey and I moved from Aiken to Granville, then Columbus, then Denver, Wyoming, Tucson, I noticed that churches had names. This puzzled me at first. Aiken's never had one, it was always just "the church." But then this discovery excited me, somewhat, and collecting the names then marvelling at their diversity became for me what you might call an obsession. At least Audrey did.

But obsession or not, I have in my list names like Third Street Bethel African Methodist Episcopal Church, Y'Our Church, Ekoji Buddhist Sangha, Primera Iglesia Pentecostal Hispana de South Tucson Arca de Salvation, Faith Hope and Charity Inc.

And these names delight me.

Inc.

How inventive the faithful can be!

And back in Aiken, we just had "the church." I suppose it doesn't much matter though, our church not having a name when there were so many to choose from. It's just a building. And then, and now, an old, empty, rotting one.

CHAPTER IX
SINGER SLANT-O-MATIC MODEL 401

It's been over two weeks now, and still no sign of my man Gonzalo. I'm beginning to worry. His stint in the civil patrol should have ended, and I've had to go through one weekend more than usual using my hands and my arms and my facial muscles to communicate with the *ladinos* from the city. Part of me wants to say I wish they'd learn English. But that's dumb, I know it, Christ. It's their country. And besides, what would you or, if this is indeed simply an extended journal entry, my descendants, think of me?

I finally asked my cook Carmela about Gonzalo, best I could—she speaks my language worse than I speak hers—but all I can get from her seems something like a How the hell should I know?

Maybe they're not related after all. Hmm.

When my father died, Bracken, Bracken, and Lodge of Mount Vernon (I think the Lodge was an in-law of one of my cousins) handled the probate. It went short, less than a month, and during that time I ran the store as usual. Of course my father would be leaving the store to me. There was no one else but his in-laws, who had done well enough for themselves with Social Security and Herman's Proctor and Gamble pension, and there were my sisters, but the place wouldn't go to them. They were out of Aiken, and no women in our history had yet kept the journals, plus to keep them you had to live in Aiken and know it and own the store and so forth.

It was during this time that I broke Audrey's heart by telling her we couldn't afford to buy the Lubbers place.

She watched the store while I went to the reading of the will, so she didn't hear what my father had left us: besides the store, its attached house, and our twenty-some remaining acres, a nice sum of cash, several thousand dollars. I guess he must have some time long ago begun planning ahead, thinking of his kids.

BETTER SAFE THAN SORRY.

That was my father. But if I were to die today—before I finish writing this sentence, for example—what would I have to leave little Moses back in Arizona? (Whew! Made it through another!)

Well, this:

1) The same store, house, and land my father left me, but with higher property taxes despite its decreased worth. Who knows how Ohio's Knox County pulled *that* off?

2) A restaurant in Tela, Guatemala, and a small house here too, both of which amount in value to something like infinitely less than the Ohio Hopkins holdings, unless Moses and his mother Audrey decide they want to live here. Carmela and Nati (dear Nati) and Gonzalo, if he ever comes back, they're all good people. But if you're not here to watch them, they'll rob you sightless (I can't blame them for it, and don't—they live better now than they did when I got here, but still...).

3) Is that old LeSabre worth anything? If Audrey and Moses haven't dumped it yet, does it count? And,

4) Two hundred-three *quetzales*—about forty bucks (I just checked my pockets), were they to decide not to live here and could be lucky enough to find a reasonably favorable exchange rate.

All told, nothing like the thousands my father left me. Not even close. Makes you wonder if the American Dream might be doing a slow fade.

In the short list above, I somehow forgot to mention the Hopkins family journals. If I were to die today, they would certainly belong to little Moses too, like it or not. Again, this that I write now, even with its quotations from my own journal entries, in addition to those of my ancestors, may or may not be part of those journals. I haven't decided. If it is, though, it'll be his as well, again like it or not. If it isn't? If I suddenly decide that this story I'm telling is worth no more than, say, the paper it's written on?

My cook Carmela can always use some kindling to fire up her stove.

The inheritance. I kept knowledge of my father's money from Audrey, an easy secret to keep with no one around to give it away, until we decided to flee Aiken. What if she wanted to buy the Lubbers's place, with its willows? She could have pressured me to do it, offering to do something sexual for me or some such. And of course that would have been money wasted. As of the time we quit, nobody from the outside had yet bought a single square inch of the property of Aiken's fleeing people. Still haven't, as far as I know, but maybe if Stevie—Steve—wins our suit the government'll come through. It's happened before. Times Beach in Missouri for instance.

Audrey didn't get angry when I told her of the money, the thousands that were ours to spend the ways we wished. Maybe she knew all along and just didn't let on.

Secrets.

The twenty acres. When George Wythe Hopkins first came to what would become Aiken, Ohio, it must have seemed that all the land was his.

...AS FAR AS THE EYE CAN SEE...

But in 1862, the Congress of the northern states, including, of course, Ohio, passed the Homestead Act, which limited (though not intending to) each person to a hundred-sixty acres, at a cost of ten dollars. That's how Audrey's ancestor Aaron Marsh got his. In 1866 they decided it didn't matter if you'd been on the other side, though Aaron never was really. My family could have claimed more, using sons and daughters, but the hundred-sixty must have seemed enough to my ancestor Benjamin Harrison Hopkins, who was running the family at the time of the Act's passing—we were merchants, not farmers.

So sometime during the War Between the States we became landowners in a limited way. Though I don't remember for sure and the journal records are iffy, I think we kept the land until my father. I'm thinking he sold a good part of it, bit by bit, and maybe that was how he'd put those thousands away.

A note on my father.

Me and Audrey's courtship, as I said, lasted barely more than a year, and during it we didn't really get to know each other very well, mostly surface stuff. We had other ga-ga eyes things to do, being in our own way new to each other and all: two toes on her right foot were very short, shorter than the others, connected by this little weird web; I had blue eyes, like the actor Paul Newman's, and if I wore a blue shirt they looked even bluer, she told me. (Her eyes, by the way, were gray, matching her hair, and in style even her thin lips at times when she didn't wear lipstick.) In the year between our wedding and my father's death, we got to know each other a little better, though my father living with us got in the way at times. I'm sure he didn't mean to, and we tried not to hold his unintended intrusion against him.

That year.

In free time, work done, Audrey often sat in my grandmother Dorothy's chair with the pole alone lighting a book in her lap.

"What are you reading?" I asked her, an August evening, cloudy, darkening early.

"Proust," she said.

"What's it about?" I'd never heard of it.

"Life," she said.

"Is that all? It looks big."

"Is. Shh."

And, another time...

"I need the truck today," she said, a sunny, unseasonably warm autumn day.

"Check with Tom."

"He doesn't care."

78

"Did you check with him?"

"He's sleeping," she said, and glanced toward the store's front window. I walked around the counter and to the screen door, looked through it without opening it. My father *was* sleeping, in one of the rockers. He looked old, and even more so because his head was tilted back and a dry leaf, it must have been September, a dry, gray leaf rested on his nose, quavering slightly and changing shades with each breath he took. His cancer hadn't yet come, but it wasn't too far distant, and somehow you knew his time must be coming.

The truck.

"Take it, I guess," I told Audrey. "Where're you going?"

"Into town." Meaning Mount Vernon, I supposed.

"What're you going for?" Was I going to have to pry for the rest of my life, pry like a snoop? At the same time that I had my own secrets to keep? I shouldn't put it that way. At the time, I felt only curious, not resentful, likely not guilty.

"You want some new slacks, don't you?"

"Let me guess," I said. "So-Fro?"

"Bingo!"

It was several months into that last couple of years in Aiken that I realized the women in my life, at least those who knew how to sew (Jane certainly excepted) and didn't mind (apparently) spending so much time doing it (it always seemed too drone-like to me to be something enjoyable), it was quite a while before I realized they actually had to buy the fabric they used.

It's not simply that I didn't know where it came from. Rather I just never thought about it. I guess with most of us, our worlds are often limited by need to know, our vision narrowed by whatever task of our own lies dead ahead.

Maybe that's not for most of us. Maybe it's just me.

I've often thought the rest of the world had a head start.

At her sewing machine, Audrey was both poet and mechanic, and is so far the only person I've met who I'm certain contradicts that dualistic thesis of Wyoming's Johnny Proctor. And though I was still with her when he made to me his gift of that philosophy, despite having her as ready evidence to refute it I, as a willing acolyte, accepted it none the less. In retrospect, I think this may have been a forest-for-the-trees thing. Whatever, now it's so ingrained, so a part of my way of seeing, that I have a hard time giving it up.

To reiterate, "There's two kinds of people in the world. You got your poets, and you got your mechanics."

Still, at least when it came to sewing, Audrey Marsh Hopkins was both.

She used a Singer Slant-O-Matic Model 401. With it and its special attachments she worked sewing miracles. She could scallop, darn, and embroider, do applique and buttonholes, raised or corded. She could sew perfect seams, corded or top-stitched, and blind-stitched hems. And with the footer attachment, she could create perfectly decorative hems, with lace or without, without basting or pressing. For the latter, she'd set the stitch selector to A and K and the red lever to 3—once I saw the creation taking place on that Singer Slant-O-Matic Model 401, I paid damn close attention. You never know when you might be witnessing a one-of-a-kind, once-in-a-lifetime performance.

With her machine's multi-slotted binder, my wife Audrey could affix any variety and design of pre-made, commercial binding. With its ruffler, she could create either gathered or pleated ruffles (same settings as above, but using the straight stitch throat plate). Using the Special Purpose Foot, she could couch, gimp, yarn, or braid stitch patterns.

Confession time.

To be honest, I paid attention, and I recall a lot, but I don't remember everything she did with her Singer, or even what she called much of it. But somehow, in the split and the divorce, I ended up with her machine's Owner's Manual—it's on the table next to my typewriter—and much of what I just related to you came directly from it. She must have been capable of doing it all though, and must have done it. She, simply put, could make and did the most durable and well-designed slacks, work pants, and shirts I've ever seen.

Consider this:

Today, more than seven years since the last time I saw her, close to a dozen since she tailored her first shirt for me, for me, her new lover and husband, most of what I still wear she styled on that Singer. It still holds up, and it so far has defied all changes in fashion over the last several years. As far as I can tell. My view from Tela is limited somewhat—by the types of American and European tourists that come to our out-of-the-way haven, by the tastes of the *ladino* boys and girls who copy, feebly or not, Europe and the United States, and by the extent of my interest, or disinterest, in it all.

As I said, Audrey on her Singer was both mechanic and poet.

To hear me talk now of my ex-wife and her sewing, you'd think I missed her.

Well.

More on that year:

"Slower?" I asked Audrey sometime late winter of that year after we married that my father still lived with us, trying my best to adjust my movement, the undulation of my hips, according to her gently and shyly offered directions. "Like this?" Despite our relative isolation there in Aiken, the need for increased sensitivity to a woman's intimate wishes wasn't lost on me. "Like this?" I repeated patiently when she only moaned in response.

"Oh, yes!" she finally cried, I thought it would never come, and I was thinking she meant it, really meant it, when through our still-thin walls thundered a "KEEP IT DOWN, YOU TWO!"

Or was it only the blaring praying cough of a dying man, not imitating his own father, not consciously begging attention, simply coughing, simply dying.

In the silence that followed, Audrey's "Oh, yes!" soundlessly echoed empty and childish. I went limp and slid out of her. We laughed together, but not together, our moment had slipped away.

Moments do that, you know.

In the year after me and Audrey's wedding, then, my father occasionally came between us. Hers didn't, of course. They had already fled for Arizona. Quickly, quietly, here one day and gone the next, since we didn't need their place they'd hang onto it, they'd said. Audrey didn't cry, and their leaving didn't seem at all to bother her. This puzzled me, and I said so:

"What gives?"

"It's not like they're dead, Jerry," she said. "We'll see them again."

She would be right, of course.

Back to my father. As I said, he soon died, and soon after—really more than a year, but it went by so quickly—soon after, Audrey and I packed up and left the Hopkins family's Aiken to make our lives, such as they were and would be, elsewhere.

CHAPTER X
BEAN EATERS

Audrey and I spent our first Christmas outside of Aiken with Granville's Karl Kohl. He managed the IGA where, after we left Aiken, Audrey worked as a cashier, me as a stocker and bagger, as a thirty-year-old carry-out boy. It was our fifth Christmas together, me and Audrey, if you count 1978, the one before we were married. And you might as well count it. We were practically living together anyway.

I had already begun to ignore the journals. Again, with no Aiken, and with no Hopkins boys on the way, I couldn't see any reason to continue keeping them. Into early winter, we had immersed ourselves in our work, purposeless and banal as it was. It was then I first realized that although to me Hopkins General Merchandise in its last failing years took more than it gave, the responsibility of running it and owning it had been in its own way an invigorating thing, life-giving, and I'd certainly miss it.

Sometimes, as Grandpa Tom might have said, YOU DON'T KNOW WHAT YOU'VE GOT TILL IT'S GONE.

My father had written some about the feeling being your own boss (not to mention keeper of the town and the family history) gave you. I only noticed it though last week, after I had already begun to write this and, to refresh my memory, was randomly flipping through pages and sections of the journals. Odd I hadn't caught that before—had I, I might have been more prepared for Granville and the IGA and Karl Kohl, for me and Audrey's first move—I've read every page and entry at one time or another, most several times. Maybe I just needed to read this particular entry with more experience gone through me. Whatever, this is what he had to say. You'll notice he mentions me in here, too. It's strange the first time you hear yourself spoken of in the third person, immortalized in another's words.

Trust me.

April 25, 1964

Steve from across the road, he and my young Jerry, they asked if they could help around here in any way today. That's the first time Jerry's shown an interest in the business. He's only twelve, I know, no, eleven going on twelve, but still I couldn't help thinking that it's about time.

I've always worked here, except for the war. For as long as I can remember, Hopkins General Merchandise has belonged to me, to me and mine. If it weren't for that war, I might say I've led a sheltered life. But I've seen others, taking orders from sergeants or lieutenants or civilian supervisors. I've watched them cower and rush to obey, take their pay and run without courage to shelters that always belonged to someone else, if not in fact, then at least in soul. These people, most people, are not whole, as far as I know.

I wish I could explain. I wish I could explain better, especially for those who will read this, Jerry will, he'll read it. I hope he'll understand someday. I hope he'll understand.

I had Jerry and the Lubbers kid scrub the gas pumps out front and wire brush the oil racks. They talked the whole time they were doing it. Who knows what about. They just beat the rain.

It's still raining, soft, quiet, constant. Jerry and Steve left right after they finished up. Ran across the road and behind the Lubbers house. Haven't seen them since. It's been a few hours.

It's late. The store's closed up for the night. Everyone's gone, June and the girls are inside. Somehow she knew I wanted some time alone, even though I myself didn't know it. She's a good woman, a damned good woman.

I'm sitting in one of the old chairs on the porch, sitting alone with the rain and somewhere across the empty highway the untrou-

bled whistle of a solitary whippoorwill.

Something ancient is running through me. It's bitter. Sweet. Blends of tastes as curious and common as cider vinegar, lime, and cactus honey, all served long hours before dawn at the same time the Melanesian musicians, with their dissonant notes still echoing off the bamboo walls, begin to put their instruments away, away into their discordant, hollow black cases.

I'm on my own God____ porch, but somehow I'm thrown out of myself, then slung back, as if by an aroma abruptly encountered that only as I name it do I realize I have mistaken it for another.

There are infinite possibilities, and I must weigh, consider, study them.

No.

There's too much philosophy already.

The world is a simpler place than that.

T.J.H.

Now that I think about it, I have noticed that entry before. I've always had some difficulty understanding it. It seems very large, and about very many things, universal things. Sure, my father wrote there some about what I said, about what owning and operating Hopkins General Merchandise meant.

But I wonder, was he also speaking here of the war? Should I have looked to this entry of April 25, 1964, to learn what World War II and his participation in it meant to him? He speaks of naming something and not being able to. Should I look here to discover what he never would, or never could, say to me directly?

Sometimes, I just don't know....

Names.

Indians used to live in the area around Aiken and Aiken's Run. As I learned back in the dead Miss What's-her-name's eighth grade Ohio history class, the European settlers of the seventeenth and eighteenth centuries, in their fear and their ignorance and their haughtiness, called them the Delawares and the Wyandots. They may or may not have called themselves something else. Without doing some kind of research, such as in Miguel Romero's Spanish-language *Encyclopedia Britannica*, and you know I can't do that, especially without Gonzalo, I have no way of knowing.

I do know though that back in Tucson the local Indians—"Native Americans," they have more recently named themselves generically—called themselves specifically the Tohono O'Odham. But for a couple of hundred years they were known to settlers irreverently, though perhaps not out of irreverent intentions, as Papagos. Roughly translated, Bean Eaters.

The Indians around Aiken, whatever their proper names, were gone by the time George Wythe Hopkins arrived, dead or run out. But our high school teacher Mr. Melvin (the Melvin whose parents sold their farm to my maternal grandparents), Mr. Melvin insisted on relating to us his students their lore, their customs, as if, despite fact as evidence to the contrary, it was all a part of our own history.

People bored with their own past, embarrassed that their own heritage seems something less than exotic, tend to do that.

Who knows why.

One of the beliefs of our predecessors in the area that Mr. Melvin apparently loved to teach—I had him for three years, thus heard it three times—was that a person's identity, rather than being limited to his physical being, included also his or her shadow, footprint, walk, dress, portrait, words. Name.

By extension, after a person died, he or she could be contacted, even brought to life, through proper communion with artifacts and remnants, by the living.

I've sometimes wondered if that's the purpose of the Hopkins family journals, to maintain somehow something more than just some mental, some faint and ethereal, communication between the living and the dead, between the past and the present. When I read an entry from an ancestor, am I actually touching more than that man's ideas, rather touching his soul, bringing it to life, to an elusive but vital life? And are my words then, my words and even the shapes that represent them, as I think them then write them then bind them to others, are they more than just rhythms, words, just stories?

Are they, more than any other of my actions, what form my identity for posterity?

Aren't they what will finally make me immortal—not in the manner of a poet whose words and ideas live more or less forever, but more in the manner, say, of in the Sonoran desert a four-inch roach-like *palo verde* bug, which when you crunch it under the heel of your boot crunches identical, presumably, to its ancestors millions of years before, but does more than recall those ancestors, actually *is* them.

I have never thought much about immortality. Thinking now though, I don't want to be immortal. Gods should be immortal. Good people, people like my mother and father, my sisters (including Jane, I suppose), they should be immortal.

Not me. At the risk of being overly self-deprecating, and tiresome being so, let me say now that I have sinned more than I can sometimes bear, and at this point I think my life would do well to end when by body does.

Christ! I hope that suicide stuff's not coming back.

Christmas at Karl Kohl's.

Audrey and I had moved months earlier from Aiken to Granville. Christmas day there, 1982, it rained some of the morning, then suddenly cleared up, brightening the homey inside of our boss Karl Kohl's house.

Karl had a wife, a fat woman with cherry cheeks and square features and a matching disposition that exaggerated an appearance already a caricature of a second-generation immigrant *Frau*. They had six children, ages ranging from seventeen down to five.

"Kitty's in the tree," Susie, the youngest, said to her father early in the afternoon, an hour or so after roast turkey and ham dinner. She had just run into the kitchen through the back door, letting it slam irritatingly being her. Karl, Helga, and I were sitting at the kitchen table, all of us sipping a thick, bitter coffee, Karl smoking his pipe. Audrey, the last time I had seen her, had been sitting surrounded by children in between the front room's fireplace and its Christmas tree (*tannenbaum*, would Karl have called it in private?). Perhaps I should have known then that Audrey was a natural mother.

"He's stuck," Susie said, with the kind of pathetic urgency only a child could express, import and urgency burning like heartbreak, "and he's scared, real scared."

Karl turned his pipe upside down over the blue Hotel Malabata Tanger ashtray, who knows where it might have come from, and tapped it a couple of times. He slid his chair back, stood slowly, and walked with his usual affected limp toward the door. "Let's just see if he'll come down for me," he said, a consoling tone despite its Prussian austerity. Then he suddenly slipped—the floor must have been wet from Susie's tracks—and went down heavily and noisily, his left hand inadequately bracing the fall. Helga squeaked her own chair backwards and rushed to him, asking him something in German over and over in a heavy whine.

He said, "I can't walk for a *damn* anymore," still lying on his back. "And for Christ's sake, speak English!" I at first stayed in my chair, thinking without time to really think that the fall was likely nothing unusual and as such they themselves would know best how to handle it. Finally, though, I felt compelled to get up and help Helga get Karl to his feet. He was heavy, as heavy as he'd always looked. Some things are indeed what they appear to be.

Susie still had her cat-up-the-tree problem.

"I'll go," I said after Karl was back in his chair. "Are you all right? Anything broken?"

"Fine, damn it."

When Helga had taken her seat as well, I slipped my shoes on and went, passing the halltree without grabbing my coat, following Susie, who had stood waiting patiently through her father's fall and recovery, out the back door. The air was cold, the damp ground soft. It all felt good, though, like a slap in the face, a wanted one, the kind that brings you to your senses.

Karl's house washed too homey, with the happy children and the perfect Christmas tree and the tasty dinner. It reminded me too much, maybe, of all we'd lost, at the same time seeming mocking of it all. I had told myself throughout the day that part of me should be, must be enjoying it all, though. Their friendliness and open, apparently unconditional compassion, towards both me and Audrey. But did they just feel sorry for us?

Pity the poor children who've lost everything.

I hated them then, for their pity and their Christmas and their children who kept Audrey in one room and me in another, kept us from doing more than exchanging glances that may or may not have indicated that we were experiencing the day the same way.

They could pity themselves. They could go fuck themselves.

"Up there," Susie whined. "See?" I didn't, at first, but I was finally able to distinguish the gray of the cat from the dull bark of a winterbare branch ten feet or so above the ground. The cat opened its mouth, white teeth against blood-red throat, as if to howl, but no sound came out.

"She is scared, isn't she?" I said. No sense blaming the kid for her parents.

"He! Kitty's a he."

"He," I corrected myself, then looked up to the cat. "You can come down now," I said, pitching my voice as if talking to a baby, to one of Rachel's twins, or both. "It's all right." The cat only blinked, and that didn't have any clear connection to what I'd said. I decided I'd have to go get him. He was clearly confused. I spied a branch about seven feet above the ground probably thick enough to hold my weight, but if I started to climb, I thought, what guarantee did I have that the cat would stay put? "You're scaring Susie, now," I said, as if I could somehow shame Kitty into cooperating. "She wants you back." From my left came suddenly an unfamiliar voice, deep but weak, lacking any resonance.

"Praying to the trees, huh?" it said. I looked and saw purply wrinkled hands gripping the top of Karl's split-rail fence, plaid flannel cuffs and shirt sleeves leading to a dingy, grease-stained hunting vest, a white stubble of a beard, tight lips, violently crimson nose, blood-shot eyes that seemed out of place even in the skull-shaped face. I didn't recognize the man. Maybe his wife did the grocery shopping.

"Cat's caught in the tree," I said. The man turned his head aside and spit green-brown tobacco juice. Some more dribbled disgustingly down his chin.

"It won't do you no good," he said. "God ain't up there."

"The cat's caught in the tree."

"Used to do it myself. Ain't gonna do you no good. You got to look inside."

I had to admit that whoever he was, wherever he had come from, he was at least partially right:

Trees are not immortal gods. They're just trees, and praying to them most certainly will not, not ever, produce results that can in any sense be considered acceptably fruitful.

As far as I know, anyway.

Susie and I eventually gave up. Soon after, we in the kitchen heard Kitty clawing her way up the back door screen, down out of the tree, hungry, come down on his own.

As to the last part of the strange man's cryptic admonishment, I don't know. Look inside for what? For what, damn it?

Some Merry Christmas.

That Christmas day was pretty much representative of me and Audrey's few months in Granville. Confusing. A bewildering world. Peopled by strange folks, some of whom had children and pets and accents and spoke in riddles. We moved into Columbus the next month, January, 1983.

Some Happy New Year.

Chapter XI
The Dead Woman

There was a commotion down at the lake this morning, and though I usually like to stay out of things that aren't my business, I let Nati talk me into going down to check it out.

She has this thing she does with her eyes—no, with her whole face, she tilts her head forward and turns her eyes, just her eyes, toward me, and she looks so innocent, I guess, maybe adoring...

Anyway, I had to follow her, how could you say no? A crowd, maybe twenty, thirty people, had gathered around one of the old piers and were watching a couple of men with hooks the size of shepherds' staves pulling a body from the water. One had fastened his hook onto the butt end of the body's skirt, a multi-colored fabric typical of the local Indians, though which Indians I of course couldn't say, especially since wet the colors blended into little more than subtly different shades of purple.

Still, after seven years here you'd think I'd have paid enough attention to be able to tell the difference. Some people, I guess, are just incorrigible in some matters.

The skirt pulled off the body, and the body returned to the water with a splash. Looked like what me and Stevie swimming back in Aiken's Run would have called a suicide dive, head and feet first striking the water simultaneously, torso last, sending cones of water high and to the sides if done correctly.

Mentally I gave him a six on form, a five for difficulty.

I say him because the body was clearly that of a man. He wore pants underneath his skirt, blue work pants like a janitor back in the states might wear. That's not unusual, understand, most men here dress that way, at least most Indians. It's one of those quaint local things that makes our country attractive to tourists.

Finally one man managed to hook onto the body's ankle, and while he held it still another found its neck, his hook not encircling it, but rather piercing it, a meat thermometer in a Christmas turkey. There was no blood. I guess the man had been dead awhile, thank goodness.

The two hauled the body up onto the pier. It lay there for a second, water forming a puddle around it, darkening the wood of the pier, then flowing in tiny rivulets over the edge and dripping back into the lake. Dust to dust, so to speak. One of the men knelt down and turned the body over onto its back. The face was bloated and bluish, but still I recognized my man Gonzalo. How could I not? We've worked side by side for all these years.

I was a bit back in the crowd, fifteen feet or so, but even from the distance I could make out a small, black hole in his forehead, as far as I could figure not made by the men with the hooks. It looked somehow older.

I'd like to say I felt agony, or at least grief. I'd lost a companion, after all, maybe even a friend of a sort. And he might have died violently. And what of his family?

I'm almost ashamed to say it, but my first thought was this:

I need to work on my Spanish.

That was just my first thought, though. And now, some hours later, I have to say something inside me *does* hurt, as it should, or at least I think it does. My eyes, though most of the day I haven't been crying, burn like cayenne up your nose. And my stomach keeps feeling like it's shrinking, contracting not quite to the point of pain, but certainly to a point of discomfort, a distressing, unavoidable discomfort.

On the other hand, I can't help thinking it's a good thing today's a weekday, not many tourists.

Dead bodies are bad for business.

Christ! It's hard when someone dies!

Nati and I stayed back in the crowd, but I figured soon enough one or both of us would have to officially identify the body, maybe even make burial arrangements. But as we stood there, her with her head buried on my chest, me with my arms around her shoulders trying to comfort her, a man, an Indian, shoved roughly by us headed toward the pier. He reached Gonzalo and the ones who had pulled him out, knelt down beside the body, touched the face.

"*Es mi hermano*," he said, loud enough that all, I assume, could hear, saying that Gonzalo was his brother. His voice held no emotion, neither did his movement. Even as he picked Gonzalo's body up and carried it off the pier, walking not towards downtown but rather along the shore in the direction, north, of the ruins of the old Hotel Tela, even as he did that, you got the impression that he felt maybe no different about Gonzalo's body from, say, a loading-dock worker lugging a bag of rice.

Funny. I'd never seen the man, at least that I could remember—I've tried all afternoon to place him, still can't—and Gonzalo never mentioned anything about a brother, and though neither of us ever talked with one another of family, you'd think if he had one in town I'd somehow know.

I don't go through life in a total sleepwalk.

Maybe the man just came in for the day. Maybe he came here looking for his missing brother.

Maybe, Dr. Hopkins, he's not Gonzalo's brother at all!

I walked Nati back to the restaurant. She cried as we walked. Just before we reached the front door, she spoke, mixing as always Spanish and English, doing it very well.

"*No puedo* work *ahora*," she said, her voice more raspy than normal, weakly deeper, as if she had somehow during this Central American summer caught a North American midwestern January cold. From the crying, I guess. "*Cierra* Daddy Rabbit's," she said. "*Para* me?"

"I'll close it," I said, how could I say no? I told her to go home, to my place, only a block or so away. She went up on tip-toes and kissed me on the cheek, the left one, then turned and left silently. I went inside and looked around. Except for Miguel Romero—Michael Roberts of Chicago—at the bar, it was empty of people. The breakfast folks—a few computer programmers from Vancouver taking their vacations together, a German couple that worked, they said, in international shipping and took part of every July off for holiday, another young couple, a young wealthy couple, come down from New Orleans to escape their city's oppressive summer heat—they had all left. I nodded towards Miguel, and over his thick glasses, not through them, he returned what may or may not have been a scowl, then I went back into the kitchen. Carmela was stirring something, stirring two-handed, so that the flesh of her thick olive upper arms shook jelly-like, stirring something in a large stockpot, the twenty-gallon, and she didn't acknowledge my entrance. I wasn't offended. She never did. My kitchen was actually *her* kitchen, not mine at all.

What was she cooking?

I don't know.

Now, seven years after I first became her boss (so to speak), I still can never decipher what she's cooking, I only know it comes out good. The customers, wherever they come from, rave.

And the spices, from their aromas, they always seem foreign, exotic, as if I've never before encountered them, maybe no one has, maybe my Carmela has just this instant invented them.

What a poet!

"Carmela," I said, then found it hard to tell her what I had to tell her. "What are you making?" I said instead, smiling, nodding toward the pot, mock-sniffing.

She looked up and didn't answer. My stalling had bought me no time.

"It's Gonzalo," I said, and Carmela kept stirring. "He's dead," I said, "*muerto*," a word I knew. "Pedro *está muerto*." She stirred, stopped to dab something out of the pot with the middle finger of her left hand, wiped it on her apron, didn't look up.

Maybe she didn't understand me, maybe I hadn't enunciated clearly.

"Dead," I said. "Pedro," I said. "*Muerto*." I realized suddenly that I hadn't said the words any more clearly, only louder, as if Carmela were deaf rather than (to me) foreign-tongued, and I felt stupid, simply stupid, then offended that the world worked that way.

Even so, Carmela, apparently oblivious to me and my words and, naturally, my feelings, stopped stirring her soup, took in each thick hand a black, ash-stained pot-holder from her work table, and slid the pot by its handles off the fire. She took a saucepan and dipped some water from the sink she always kept half full for the purpose, and poured the water slowly through the stove top and onto the fire. It hissed loudly and steamed wet and hot and quickly made the kitchen sauna-like.

"Go home," I told Carmela. "A casa." But by the time I said it she already had her apron off and was leaning out the window shaking it free of crumbs, and I knew that I'd made myself understood in spite of myself, and that too she was closing up the kitchen—and thus the restaurant, I can't cook—without my say-so, though of course I was going to say so. And I was upset for a second but then I remembered. I owned the kitchen as I owned all of Daddy Rabbit's, but it was really hers, I knew that, and besides, this was about our dead friend Gonzalo, not about who had control over what or over whom.

Carmela hung her apron on the nail by the back door, kicked a bare foot at a stray dog that had just poked its hungry snout through it. The dog yipped and scooted, and she stood for a second, her back to me. Her head dropped forward, and her thick shoulders shook, short spasms but solid, and I touched my right hand to her left shoulder, squeezed, she leaned into it, then silently slipped—not an easy task for a woman her size—out the back door and, presumably, went home. I wiped the hot cold sweat from the back of my bald head, then closed and latched the door behind her.

Maybe Carmela and Gonzalo are—were!—related after all.

Hell. I don't know.

Death.

In the apartments Audrey and I lived in during our brief stay in Columbus, the ones with the lousy water pressure and the lisping Norma and her dog Red (and "God, talking to you"), in those apartments off Bryden Road next to St. Ann's Hospital, there lived at the same time we did, two doors down, a very large woman. She spent most of her days that spring, 1983, sitting on the top step of her porch, always eating or drinking something, smoking whenever she was eating or drinking or not, coughing constantly and heavily, spitting, waving at us when we would pass within her field of vision going in or out of our apartment.

And, we assumed, dying.

This woman when she drove drove an old Ford station wagon (we still had the '67 pick-up). She didn't work—Norma had told us that—and her only brother came over twice a week to take out her garbage, once to do her laundry, and once her grocery shopping (Norma again). We couldn't figure, then, where she went when she went. But go she did, every couple of days or so, and upon returning, though our parking spaces were all straight-in head-first, she always parked at a herringbone angle taking up a space and a half, sometimes two. She didn't do that on purpose, now, as far as we could tell—more than once we cracked our kitchen-window blinds and through their slats watched her park. She simply didn't have the strength in her arms, or the sense in her head, to be able to park correctly.

It may seem that me and Audrey were a bit on the nosy side, like a couple of old women with nothing better to do than to peeping-Tom themselves into other people's business. We didn't mean to do that. Columbus is a pretty good-sized city, and remember, it was our first one. So many things were new to us. We wanted to see.

Anyway, if our large neighbor had ever hit the pick-up pulling in or out, she wouldn't have done much damage to it. It was old then and pretty sturdy, built, you might say, like a truck. Still, we tried as often as we could to park at the other end of the lot from her. Why take chances?

One day this woman, Catherine, she left and didn't come back. First for a day, then for two, then for a week. We noticed because, of course, when coming or going ourselves we were in the habit of looking for her car so we could park, as I said, as far away from it as possible.

Suddenly it wasn't there.

And after we noticed that, at nights we would look for lights in her apartment, for some sign of life. There were none, and at some point we realized too that we hadn't seen her brother that week.

What else could we assume but that somehow, somewhere, our large neighbor Catherine had died? Had a heart attack behind the wheel, maybe, driving to who knows where. Not, finally, getting there. She became for us by the end of that week not Catherine, not our large neighbor, but rather, admittedly irreverently, the Dead Woman.

"Seen the Dead Woman lately?" I might ask Audrey when I got home from the hardware store even before I had my shoes off.

Or, "Think the Dead Woman's brother'll ever come for her stuff?" Audrey might say over dinner, just idly making conversation.

Or, "Audrey! The Dead Woman just drove up!"

She came back to the apartments after about ten days gone. Just taking a vacation (though a vacation from what I couldn't say), Norma told us as soon as she found out. But still, when Audrey and I spoke of her (not *to* her, of course), she was, and always would be, the Dead Woman:

"Where do you think the Dead Woman went?" I might say, just idly making conversation.

Or, "That's just the Dead Woman's brother," Audrey might tell me when I'd be awakened from an afternoon nap by a revving engine and begin to noisily threaten whoever might have such gall.

Or, from both of us, guiltily:

"We should be nicer to the Dead Woman."

Over the past few weeks, while Gonzalo's been gone, I think I've told myself that like the Dead Woman, he'll turn up soon enough, extending if asked an easy, obvious explanation for his lengthy disappearance. Of course, he won't be able to explain anything now. But somebody knows, knows where he's been, knows what happened to him.

Somebody knows.

When Carmela left, I double-checked that the fires were out, I closed and latched the kitchen windows' shutters, then I went back out front. Nobody new had come in, but Miguel was still sitting at the bar.

"I'm closing up," I told him as I walked through the dining room to the front door. "You want to sit a while?" I looked back at him, and without waiting for him to answer, I closed the door and locked it, the metal of the eye and hook cold to my fingertips. I decided to leave the shutters on the windows facing front, facing *Avenida* Santander, open for the breeze. I stood for a second, and heard Miguel behind me shuffle his bar stool back. I took a deep breath, then turned, and he was walking in his squeaky sneakers over to my table in the room's far southwest corner, the table where I normally sit and oversee the operation, greet and make small talk with the customers. He sat down. "Have a seat," I said, clever man, hiding whatever emotion I might have felt.

"Be glad to."

I went back behind the bar and got myself a beer from the reach-in, a Moza, dark, strong. "You need another?" I said to Miguel.

"Can't dance," he said, "too wet to plow," and he quickly tilted his head back, drained whatever he had left, and tossed the empty like a hand grenade to me across the room and then the bar. I caught it, but just barely, dropped it casually into the return carton, then went out and joined him. "What's up?" he said, then turned his head to the side and burped quietly into his cupped hand. "I've never seen you close so early but for a holiday. Somebody die or something?"

"Gonzalo."

"Mmm."

"They just dragged him out of the lake."

"Funny," he said. "Most of the natives around here swim like fish. Other 'ords, it's in their blood."

"He didn't drown. Looked like he'd been shot. Through the head, right between the eyes."

"Too bad," Miguel said, and took his glasses off, wiped them with the tail of his t-shirt (red with *Go Fuck the Canyon* printed across the front— he could be a real jerk). "It's gonna be a hot one today."

"He didn't have any enemies, far as I know. How about you? You've been here longer than I have." A couple of years longer, nine to my seven, but both of us have lived in Guatemala long enough that a couple of years doesn't make any difference. Still I always, for some reason, show some deference to Miguel when it comes to things native. He always seems so sure of himself on such matters, and I for some reason often stay unsteady, like ice-skating blind on a creek other than Aiken's Run.

Miguel hadn't answered. "Did he?" I said. "Have any enemies?"

"Christ," Miguel said. "For all I know he was a fuckin' rebel, a fuckin' terrorist."

"Gonzalo?" I said, stunned at first, but then for a moment thinking he was just kidding. "Are we talking about the same guy?"

"You can't tell by lookin', Jerry. Other 'ords, don't be so naive."

I took a good swallow of beer, leaned back in my chair, leaned the chair on back on two legs till my head touched the wall. I closed my eyes and didn't say anything.

"Christ," Miguel continued unprompted, "he might've been runnin' drugs through here for all you know, a regular fuckin' Pablo Escobar, drugs, or guns, for all you know. Guns for the rebels. Damn it, Jerry, we don't need the fuckin' rebels around here, you know they're bad press, bad for the country, Christ, bad for business, *your* business, you ought to know that."

I opened my eyes and turned them to him, but still held my silence. I suddenly didn't feel like talking, wished I'd sent him out with Carmela.

"They deserve what they get," he went on. I'd heard him rant before, naturally, but rarely so much, something must have really gotten his adrenaline going this time. "You let 'em keep fuckin' around, makin' news, next thing you know we got UNPROFOR, the fuckin' United Nations. Remember Lebanon? How about Yugoslavia? You been payin' attention? We don't *need* UNPROFOR comin' in. Fuckin' Italians or Pakistanis shootin' themselves in the foot. Fuckin' Americanos with 'em, with their cameras and their news, their goddamned news, their goddamned left-wing, terrorist-glorifying news."

"It's just Gonzalo," I said, "could have been any of us," and I noticed as he lifted his bottle of beer to his mouth that his hand was shaking, trembling not quite violently, but still you knew he was holding something back. It was a bit scary.

"Nothing's just anything," he said.

A woman, a white woman, European or American, not Guatemalan, not *ladino*—they only come on the weekends—a woman poked her head through one of the windows, looking toward the inside lock on the front door, appearing confused, maybe wondering if she'd read the brochure wrong, if maybe she'd missed the part about siestas, which of course we don't do here, that's a Spanish thing. From Spain. Across the ocean.

"Closed," I said. "A death in the family." She just stared at me, cocking her head slightly, still looking perplexed.

"Fuckin' joint's closed!" yelled Miguel, and the woman disappeared, quick as a wind sprint.

I said, "Maybe it's too early for you to be drinking, buddy," and without another word Miguel Romero—Michael Roberts—stood up and himself bolted towards the window, deftly slipped through it, right arm and leg first, then vanished. I haven't seen him again all day.

Some people.

I used someone's death to my advantage once.

One day in January of 1983, after Audrey and I had already decided that Granville and its Karl Kohl and its IGA weren't for us, one day, a Sunday, I was scanning the want ads in the *Columbus Dispatch* for some way to support us when we moved. All I could find, all I felt remotely qualified for, were jobs similar to the IGA thing I'd be leaving: grocery or convenience-store, low wage, no future, no brain or experience required. Okay, maybe, for a sixteen-year-old, but depressing, not to mention emotionally catastrophic, for someone my age at the time. After a couple of hours with the want ads, then, I did the natural thing for someone in such a desperate, dismal, joyless state. I turned to the obituaries.

There I found that a man named Jimmy Jones Jenkins had the day before tragically passed away, suddenly, only 48 (heart attack? cancer?), survived by his wife Mae and two daughters, three grandchildren, life-long member East Side Lions Club, member V.F.W. Post 39__, funeral today 2:00, Blacklick American Baptist, burial at Woodlawn Cemetery. But before all that, and by far the most important fact included:

> At the time of his death, Mr. Jones served as Assistant
> Manager with Davidson Hardware.

The next day, I took the truck into Columbus, located this Davidson Hardware on the near east side, and confidently, after determining that the manager (not a German this time, but rather a Hungarian, an apparently stolid, for he seemed quick to smile so near his assistant manager's sudden death, an apparently stolid Hungarian named Gary Gombos), after determining that the manager was working in paints today, I confidently presented myself as an experienced hardware man offering his knowledge and experience in return for permanent employment. Gary hired me on the spot, Audrey and I came back in and found our apartment near St. Ann's the next day, and by the following Monday we had left another town, another home, behind.

Nati is in the other room, sleeping in my bed. The rising then falling racket the civil patrols make as they drive into town and down the *Avenida* toward some lakeside destination has come and gone. I'm writing by flickering candlelight and have been for the last hour or so. From time to time I let the generator run out of fuel. I have a different generator for Daddy Rabbit's, and I never let it fail. Perishables. Maybe when it comes to things more personal, I'm just lazy.

The candlelight flickers, moves the shadows from my hand and my pen back and forth across my words and across the blankness which will hold my words, because my house, like all buildings here in Tela, isn't airtight. The planks that form the walls touch only randomly, windows have no glass, the shutters that closed cover them, cover them only barely. Some people who visit our town for the first time have trouble with this. Privacy, they say. Most get used to it.

As I said, I still haven't seen Miguel. He lives next door at times, remember, and though his house is surrounded thickly by croton and bamboo and hurricane fence, stars of light sprinkle through nights he's there. It has stayed dark all evening. Wasn't he a strange bird today.

The whole day has felt dreamlike strange.

Sometimes I feel like my whole life has been the same way.

I'm wondering now if I announce Gonzalo's death in Tuesday's *La Prensa Libre de Tela*, and if I make certain that the announcement mentions his position with Daddy Rabbit's, will some nicely qualified multilingual mechanic show up to casually, shamelessly, replace him?

CHAPTER XII
UNCLE FRED'S QUICK LIQUID RAT POISON

So far in my life, I've never almost died.

The closest I came came during me and Audrey's few months in Columbus.

We moved to Columbus in January and lived there till late spring, end of May, first of June. We lived in the apartment I've mentioned, in a way gathering dust, but in another discovering, naively, I suppose, but still with a tentative confidence, some kind of direction for ourselves.

I discovered, for example, that hardware was definitely not my calling.

"I need one of those, those uh...you know?" said a customer, a burning cigar sticking out from between his teeth and bobbing up and down as he talked.

"You can't smoke in here, sir," I said, forever polite. "Paint. Toluene." Other chemicals."

"Sorry," he said, but he made no move to put it out. "It's shaped like this, and about so big?" With the fat index fingers and thumbs of both hands he made nothing more than a three-inch circle.

"What do you use it for?" I said.

"On the wall. You know."

"Metal?" I said, trying to practice my dead father's patience. "Plastic?"

He only made a face that hinted at constipation. I still had no idea what he might be looking for.

I heard Gary Gombos's commanding voice coming up behind me. "Did Jerry show you where the switchplates are, Mr. Hornberger?" Which of course, I hadn't. Why hadn't he just told me straight out what the hell he wanted? No. No. He had to make these vague finger signs like some real-life Tonto, only instead of being scripted by some Hollywood bozo to look and act like a simpleton, this guy was the real thing. And I ended up, in front of the boss, looking the stooge.

I had found, in just a few short months, the world to be more populated than I could have ever imagined with these Grandpa Hermans. Aiken hadn't been like that. We'd had our one, and I'd seen more of him than most people, us being related and all. But you could get used to one, especially when you'd had so many years of your father showing you how to do it.

And, like the rest of the world, we'd had our share, in the same fifty-fifty or so ratio, of Proctor's poets and mechanics. But in Aiken, even the most tool and equipment-illiterate of the poets could name a god-damned switchplate!

Sounds trivial now, looking back. I guess my patience was wearing thin, my fuse shortening, my nerves fraying (my clichés multiplying?).

Perhaps I was homesick. If so, with no home left now, with that homesick itch unscratchable, it might be understandable that I'd get a bit dejected, and that my dejection would manifest itself first, perhaps most prominently, in anger. Then in other more destructive, more self-destructive ways.

That last seemed to be happening. Back at Hopkins General Merchandise we had carried an Uncle Fred's Quick Liquid Rat Poison. One day at Davidson Hardware, which carried it also, I rediscovered that Uncle Fred's contained arsenic. As I left work on May 24, 1983, I bought a can. Gary looked at me funny, kind of cocked his head, raising one eyebrow higher than the other. Did he know what I had in mind?

"That doesn't draw them out, you know," he said. "You've got to know where they come in then put it in their path." I handed him a five, a crisp one, and he took it, in one hand wrinkled it up while he made change with the other. "You make them think it's water."

"Oh," I said, "we don't have any rats." He lay the wrinkled bill in the till, closed the drawer, then did the eyebrow trick again. I said, "I've found it works well on mice too," though we didn't have those either. If we had, Audrey certainly would have said something by now. She had never been real talkative, of course, and in those days in Columbus she had become even less so, as if she too were suffering her own depression and knew it would be useless to try talking about it with someone so obviously self-centered as I was.

Still, something like mice she would have mentioned.

She liked them. Especially the babies, the knuckle-sized, nipple-pink bald babies. Once back in Aiken, at Hopkins General Merchandise some had turned up in a drawer behind some white corrugated boxes of flat-head screws. She had found them.

"I'll get the Uncle Fred's," I'd said.

"Let's leave them alone," she'd answered, her voice soft and caring like an old chamois. "They won't hurt anything."

"But they're mice," I'd said, quickly realizing that the term *mice* likely had a different meaning for me than it did for her.

"Exactly," she said. Instant confirmation. "Look how cute."

So if we had mice at the Bryden Road apartment, Audrey certainly would have said something. And if we had them, she also certainly would have noticed. During our time in Columbus, Audrey never worked outside "the home," what home it was. Three rooms and a shower. Radiator heat that in the winter and spring shut on or off at random, of its own accord, keeping us cold on cold days and hot on warm ones. One window in each room, all four windows no more than a yard square, so on those warmer spring days when we might open the windows to a breeze, all we could do was hear it whooshing through the tops of the property's oaks and pines, no breeze could come inside. The place stayed still and stuffy.

The kitchen had a very small stove with four burners, of which only two worked. The refrigerator needed to be defrosted almost weekly.

The water you've heard about.

We'd brought a television, but we'd never spent much time watching it and didn't start then, and a radio kept tuned to WOSU, to public radio and classical music. Depressing fare itself for the most part.

Only Audrey's Singer Slant-O-Matic seemed to give her much joy in those days, but the joy it gave her must certainly have been limited. She could only make so many curtains, slacks, shirts, and blouses before she ran out of things to do.

And while Audrey spent her time at that apartment, I passed a good deal of mine at Davidson Hardware. Audrey and I had worked together at Karl's IGA and at the store in Aiken before that. We had never, in our few years as a couple, spent so much time away from each other. It's easy to see now how she might have mistaken my depression and dejection over the homesickness, if that's what it indeed *was* over—genes, again, may have played a part, or residue from living for so many years downstream from the weapons plant—it's easy to see how she might have mistaken it for something else. She likely just thought, for example, that I missed her all those forty or fifty or more hours a week I spent away, away at Davidson Hardware.

Audrey looked for work for a while. Cashier was a logical thing, and she applied first at one of the grocery chains, then at a department store downtown. The grocery store was in our neighborhood, a block or two south, but she took the bus to the department store, first to apply, then to interview. Both times I had to work. Like me, she had never ridden a bus before, not even a Greyhound or a Trailways, of course not a city bus.

"They're full of poor folks, Jerry," she told me over dinner—fried pork chops, mashed potatoes and gravy, cream-style corn—the evening of the first day's ride, back in mid-March. "You've never seen so many poor folks in one place."

"I've noticed them myself," I said. "Waiting at the stops on the way to work." I shoveled to the side of my plate a small mound of potatoes, forked some corn onto it, covered it all with a spoonful of steaming gravy. I lifted a bite to my mouth. "Sad, isn't it?" I said, then continued eating.

"It worries me."

"Why?"

"What if we end up that way?"

"We won't, honey," I said. I hadn't yet told her of my father's money, wondered then if maybe I should. "We're not those kind of people." I noticed she wasn't eating, but just staring at her plate and moving the food around on it, back and forth, mixing it together, mixing the already bland colors until they were becoming a mostly uniform brown the color of milk chocolate, a brown broken by occasional stones of yellow and gray points of bone. I don't know what it looked like. Maybe the primordial soup from which life first sprang on Earth. Maybe lava from a

later, modern-day volcano. No, something less exotic. The canal immediately following a downpour during Aiken's final years. Dirty, fouled,
might as well have been a landfill, depressing. "We're not like those," I
said.

She stopped stirring but still didn't look up. "They're like Norma,"
she said, speaking of our next-door neighbor. "Only they're mostly black
folks. And we live in the same place she does."

"It's only temporary," I said. "Aren't you hungry?"

"Try riding the bus sometime. You feel just like them. Poor. I don't
want to end up like them, Jerry."

"We won't," I said. "It's only temporary," I repeated, like I knew what
I was talking about. But I didn't know anything except that we had a few
thousand dollars in the bank between us and them, between our state
and theirs, and that when you didn't have a job you liked and probably
weren't good at, and you didn't have a home of your own or much family left to fall back on, money could go quickly.

I didn't know anything anymore.

Audrey didn't get hired, either at the grocery store or at the department store. Maybe with her gray hair she looked to them older than her
age, I know potential employers could be more blatant about that then
than in more recent years. Maybe she just didn't present herself well.
Those were sad days somewhat, and she might have found it hard to
show that rare and genuine smile, those dimples low on her cheeks that
always made you think that to touch her face would shoot contentment
and happiness back through your fingers and into your own very soul.

Who knows?

Whatever, by the end of March she had decided to advertise in the
Dispatch for professional-quality tailoring done in the home. Nice that
she still had at least that piece of self-confidence. She advertised, then,
and through April and up until that third week in May, she was doing
two or three jobs a week, fifteen, twenty-five, fifty dollars, alterations for
someone who'd put on forty pounds unexpectedly or for a bride-to-be
whose mother was insisting, despite a four-inch difference in their
heights, that her grandmother's dress had been good enough for her, and
it would be good enough for her daughter.

The use to which she was able to put her Singer Slant-O-Matic helped Audrey believe, I suppose, that she was doing her part to ward off that dreaded poverty. To me it all seemed a mistake, it seemed something beneath her, like the cashier job in Granville had been and the ones in Columbus had she landed them would have been. And the mistake could be traced to one person's ineptness.

Me.

Or mine. I still don't even know which word to use. Imagine how I must have felt then.

May 24, 1983, then, I bought a can of Uncle Fred's Quick Liquid Rat Poison, brought it home, and sat for a few minutes in the truck looking at it, tossing it up and down a few inches or so, letting the flat can land splat and cold in the palm of my hand. I guess trying to get a feel for how much canned death might weigh, maybe wondering if I was getting my money's worth. Finally I slipped it into the pocket of my forest green Davidson Hardware windbreaker, carried it inside unmentioned past Audrey. She apparently had fallen asleep on the couch, a fifteen-dollar burgundy, right-angled, fifties-style monstrosity from the Association for Retarded Citizens thrift store over on Mound Street next to Rollerland. She had been reading. She still read often, avidly, and had recently moved away from translations of thick and deep European writers from early in the century and toward, of all things, murder mysteries. On her chest, moving up and down slowly with her silent breath, lay *Death of a Dude*, "a Nero Wolfe Novel by Rex Stout," the cover said. Now whatever could *that* be about? I figured that, as with most of what Audrey read, I'd never know, and I went quietly by her and back to the bedroom closet. There I tucked the Uncle Fred's away in the top box of the Hopkins family journals, the most recent ones, the ones in which I hadn't made any entries for going on a year.

That night, after dinner, we read. While she stayed with Nero Wolfe, I did the newspaper front to back, the obituaries, even on my own last day, still my favorite part of the paper. We lay in bed and read, and Audrey, warm, soft, cold, hard, I didn't know why such dissonance, but naturally I blamed myself, Audrey, thanks to her daytime nap, took a long time to fall asleep. But I outwaited her. I had a mission, a meeting

with the most active ingredient in Uncle Fred's Quick Liquid Rat Poison.
I lay with my eyes closed feigning sleep, both listening to and feeling in
my chest against her back her breathing, waiting for it to turn slow and
steady, relaxed, knowing with confident resignation I was hearing and
feeling it all for the last time.

I had thought it all out. I would take the can from the closet, sneak
into the bathroom, strip naked, sit in the empty tub, then drink the
Uncle Fred's, down it all. Any mess, any bowel or stomach evacuation,
would be easy, relatively speaking, to clean up. The Brackens back in
Mount Vernon would bury me. Audrey, free from the burden of her
worthless husband, could move in, at least for a while, with her parents,
retired by now, as I said, out in Arizona. The secret money would provide for the burial (at cost, I assumed), for her move west, and for her
basic needs until she found someone else, someone more worthy, someone less a homeless loser.

In Arizona, likely some cowboy, I thought. What else were there?

No, not a cowboy. Cowboys were drifters. Rodeo to rodeo, dusty one-
horse town to dusty one-horse town. The songs I'd heard snatches of
between stations on the truck's radio said so. Drifters. Homeless.

Born somewhere else, I could be a cowboy.

Rancher. She'd find a rancher, a grizzled, self-made survivor who just
happened to own a couple of hundred thousand prime Arizona acres
(whatever those might be—I'd never seen Arizona at the time) and a few
thousand head of some special breed of cattle. Audrey would bury me
at the church, then she'd move out west and in with her parents. And
she'd meet a rancher, the self-confident and settled kind of man she
deserved. And she would marry him. And she'd be all right. She would
be fine, if she could put up with the boots.

I'd put it all in the note, leave nothing out.

The note, I thought as I lay next to Audrey. I needed to write the note.
And as I lay beside her, ready as a man could be to end his own life, feeling her finally fall asleep, I knew suddenly that I had deceived myself. I
couldn't write the note. My sister Jane was the poet. Not me. I was, if
anything, the mechanic of the remaining Hopkins family (though again
even that was far from certain). I couldn't write a suicide note and give
it the elegance, the precision such a piece of writing would need if it were

to be understood correctly, understood as the work of a man giving in to the inevitable, giving in not as a coward, but rather as a man joyfully sure of the mission his life had asked of him. But no, I wasn't sure, and no, I couldn't write, and, both disappointed and relieved, I lay next to my wife Audrey figuring that, if I was to be honest, to live up to whatever shadowy revelation that'd just come over me, come morning I had some explaining to do.

The next morning, as we drank coffee and ate breakfast and I wiped more sleep from my eyes than usual, I told Audrey about my father's money. As I said, she didn't get angry, she might have known all along. Emboldened, I told her as well about the Uncle Fred's Quick Liquid Rat Poison, still hidden in a box in the closet, atop the most recent of the Hopkins family journals.

"You're not happy at the hardware store, are you?" she said, still not angry, not even pitying, just being herself.

"No," I said. "I'm not."

And she suggested I leave the job, that the two of us load my father's F-100 back up, leaving the couch behind if we had to, and head west. Or somewhere like it, somewhere new.

"We don't really have anywhere to be, do we?" she said. "Is there anything keeping us here, anyone expecting us?"

"No," I said, and I myself smiled and agreed that a move was in order, if not "a move" then at least a road trip, and I felt the warmth of her across our table and our coffee and wheat toast, and I took a bite of that toast and I laughed uncontrollably. As I laughed, I spilled crumbs onto my chin and into my lap, and my laugh must have been genuine and as genuine infectious, because Audrey was suddenly laughing too, those dimples dancing low on her cheeks, her eyes suddenly alive like I hadn't seen for months and months, she was laughing too.

Damn it.

My Audrey was laughing too.

PART II

Where this lake is, there was a lake,
where these black pine grow, there grew black pine.

Where there is no teahouse, I see a wooden teahouse
and the corpses of those who slept in it.
—Carolyn Forché
"The Garden Shukkei-en"
from *The Angel of History*

One day in August a man disappeared.
—Kobo Abé
The Woman in the Dunes

CHAPTER XIII
HORACIO AND ALDOUS

The morning after they pulled Gonzalo's body from the lake, I awoke early, for me. The sun was up but still hadn't risen enough to cast shadows through the trees, the croton, and the windows into the house. I washed up, brushed my teeth—we use simple baking soda here, simple Arm & Hammer—soaped my head then ran the cold safety razor quickly over it. I toweled off, then dressed in my usual blue jeans, rainbow-colored *camisa*, and sandals, no socks. I felt comfortable, or as comfortable as I could, considering the circumstances.

I had slept in the front room down on the couch, and before I left I checked on Nati, asleep up in my bed. I opened the bamboo door carefully and slowly so as not to awaken her. It squeaks sometimes. She moved slightly, her left arm and right leg only, moaned a bit, a low, sexy moan. I longed to touch her, but I closed the door without entering. I needed to go clean up Daddy Rabbit's, ready it for business, do that little extra—scrub the floors back and front, defrost and rotate all the coolers—do what until a couple of weeks before had been Gonzalo's work in preparation for the weekend.

It had rained sometime overnight, sometime after I'd fallen asleep writing, sometime after I'd awakened who knew when to smother the candles and check on Nati then return to lay on the couch for the rest of the night. If it had rained earlier, I would have heard, or at least smelled the rain.

As I walked up the alley toward the *Avenida* Santander, I stepped around the occasional puddles which spotted it, oddly feeling myself to be dancing. At the intersection of the alley with *la avenida* I stopped, lit a Rubio, and stared up the barren cobblestone avenue toward Daddy Rabbit's. It held oily puddles, multitudes of both natural and somehow unnatural colors. I recalled the way back in Aiken a rain brought a refreshing look, smell, and feel, not like this. This morning Tela felt not like a town through whose streets one would dance, but rather it struck me as dirty, polluted, desecrated. It is these kinds of discrepancies between then and now, between worlds so different but in many ways the same, that make me question at times my powers of recollection, even of perception.

I usually wait until sometime during my first cup of coffee to light a cigarette, again I've only recently taken up smoking. But that morning the smoke in my lungs felt good, satisfying, I suppose, satisfying the craving my body has been developing for it. I'm not sure how I feel about that now, that dependence.

By the time I reached Daddy Rabbit's, Carmela had already opened up, of course. Standard operating procedure (the way Miguel Romero/ Michael Roberts might term it) on weekdays. She could easily wait on the few customers and cook their food as well.

I figured the time as I entered to be only about eight or so. The windows were swung open front and back, and a cooling breeze came through. A sole customer, a man I hadn't seen before, white and likely American or Canadian but possibly not, sat long and thin and hook-nosed hunched over the bar, apparently nursing a cup of coffee. I nodded, he gazed back blankly, and wondering if I was seeing myself I went back into Carmela's kitchen. She stood at the stove tossing the chopped remnants of some green-leafed spice into the twenty-gallon pot. Creating the day's soup, I supposed, what magic might she be working through her sadness? I kissed her on her plump, rocky, hairy cheek. She seemed to smile as she leaned her face into mine, but she didn't look up so I didn't know for sure.

I wish I knew her better.

As I knew I'd have to, I mopped the floors. Out front and in back both. The manual sense of it all, the resistance of the tile to the soaked and heavy weaved cotton strands of the mop, felt comforting to my hands and my heart, reminiscent of my youthful and innocent days back at Hopkins General Merchandise. The task reminded me too that those toiling hands were likely more those of a mechanic, and not necessarily a very good one, than of a poet.

Sometimes, especially lately, I'm still not certain how I feel about that either.

As I worked, as I made every effort to simply put one piece of whatever task in front of the other as mindlessly as possible, I realized that with my friend and employee Gonzalo's death I suddenly had a mystery on my hands:

Though he may at some time during his disappearance have been serving with the civil patrols, Gonzalo likely hadn't died in the line of duty. Skirmishes between the patrols and rebels are rare these days, and those that do occur as such rarely go unreported. Despite dangers of deadly reprisals, too many people I know have too much personal involvement to keep inquisitive entanglements secret.

That Gonzalo might not have died in his capacity as a member of the civil patrols doesn't mean that he wasn't the victim of some military or political or even paramilitary group. They're numerous in these highlands, and Gonzalo had no other enemies, as far as I know.

Also—and I have to admit that speaking, even writing of this makes me for maybe the first time during my residency in Tela pretty damned nervous—former CIA operative Miguel Romero's behavior had been and has been suspicious, nervous and erratic itself, especially regarding Gonzalo's death. Could be something's up. Who knows what.

I wish I'd paid more attention back when Audrey, in the couple of months before we'd left Columbus and in the few months following, on the road and then in Denver, had been reading all those Nero Wolfe mysteries. I remember the narrator as a man with a photographic memory, a man named Archie Goodwin, and I remember that the character Wolfe was a large fellow who grew flowers of some sort and never left his house. But I remember little else, least of all how he solved whatever mysteries came his way. If I did, if I had simply paid more attention to Audrey when she was trying so hard to share her reading with me, then maybe answers to the questions that to others must seem so obvious would be more apparent to me.

I might have some idea of the kinds of clues to look for, where to look, even the kinds of things concerning Gonzalo's death I don't know.

At Daddy Rabbit's that morning, I finished the floors, then stocked the beer coolers with Gallo and Moza and Monte Carlo. The coolers didn't need defrosting after all. Nati came in about eleven, lovely Nati dressed in a bright, multi-colored knee-length wrap. The dress left her brown shoulders bare, and she had her iridescent black hair piled up on her head and held in place apparently by a sole, inch-thick silver barrette at the back. A mostly red *bolsa*, a large purse, hung loosely over her right shoulder. She smiled, I predictably melted, and she immediately began the business of opening the bar, slicing limes and filling mixers and such. I grabbed a warm Moza and took my seat at my table in the room's southwest corner.

I had planned to take a break, a mindless break with no thought of Gonzalo. Perhaps I'd watch Nati for a while, perhaps I'd eventually get around to visiting the bank to get change for the weekend. Definitely at some point I'd have to make arrangements to have fuel delivered for the generator back at the house. But within a couple of minutes, still some time before whatever lunch crowd we might have was due to arrive, I had a not-so-unexpected visitor—the chief, *el jefe*, of our local police, a man named Horacio Quiñones. "*Qué tal, Senor* 'opkins?" he said from the street, leaning through the window, his face black in shadow with the almost blinding sunshine behind it, but his voice recognizable. A voice low but not deep, sharp-edged like his brother Enrique's, the primary announcer and DJ on Tela's only radio station.

"Come join me, Horacio." I absent-mindedly raised my beer towards him in a toast. He disappeared for a second then reappeared in the door-way. He entered, and with him now out of shadow I could see he was dressed in his usual police garb: khaki uniform and matching cap, Sam Brown belt with a revolver on his hip, brightly polished black boots. As he walked towards my table, I stood up. Horacio was tall for an Indian, nearly my height. Perhaps he was half, or at least part, *ladino*. I didn't know him well, so I didn't know. He offered his hand, and I shook it. I said, "You're here about Gonzalo?"

"You might offer me some coffee before we get around to business," he said, then took the seat at my table nearest the door.

I fetched some coffee for him from behind the bar. I was standing next to Nati, who was draining milk from some fresh coconuts, and as I poured Horacio's coffee she reached her hand down and squeezed my thigh. "*Te quiero*," she whispered, and despite my semi-illiteracy in the language I certainly knew what that meant. God, what grief had made me forsake the night before!

"Cream, Horacio?" I yelled over my shoulder. "*Leche?*"

"Black will be fine," he returned. I left Nati and joined him, taking my usual seat. He reopened the conversation:

"Gonzalo," he said. "Full name, Gonzalo Méndez Paredes?"

"Is this an interrogation?"

"And why do you ask?"

I must have been thinking of the states, with their Constitution and Bill of Rights and so forth, the Miranda ruling.

Whoops. Wrong country.

"No reason," I said. "I believe that was his full name."

"And he worked for you, correct?"

"Yes, of course,"

Again, I didn't know Horacio Quiñones well. He had held his position since before my arrival in Tela, over seven years ago, but contrary to what you might think, he never came around looking for payoffs, payola, offering protection either from thugs or from government regulation. He ran *la policía* with only himself and his brother Emilio as officers, and to tell you the truth, over the years I hadn't seen either of them more than half a dozen times a year. I have no idea what they did with themselves, but they had always left me quite alone.

That's one of the very nice things about doing business here in Tela. I've heard it said that the writer Aldous Huxley, who had somehow heard of our glorious Lake Atitlán, visited us once, in the early 1930s, and found Tela, according to the speaker, a "squalid, uninteresting place, with a large low-class Mestizo population and an abundance of dram shops." That may have been so then, may be now. But I'll tell you one thing. You keep to yourself, you buy from the right people, you employ locals—and you remember it's their country, not yours—and you do business in peace.

Someone like Horacio Quiñones, chief of police, remains a virtual stranger.

Back to him.

"He worked for you how long?" he continued. I had to admire his English, spoken with only a trace of an accent.

"Since 1985," I said. "Since I first came here. Where did you learn English?"

"Seven years, then?"

"Yes."

"When was the last time you saw him?"

I thought, but since I'd spent considerable time writing of my life the past couple of weeks, and since Gonzalo's been a part of my life and thus that story, I didn't have to think hard. "It's been about two weeks," I said. And the date of his first non-appearance had been an American holiday. "Since July third, a Friday," I said. "That makes what, three weeks?"

"Your math seems correct," Horacio said. "Why did you not report him missing?"

"Well," I said, "he wasn't missing. He just didn't show up." I told him, and he listened as if he didn't already know, about the once-a-month stints in *las patrullas civiles*. "Did you learn English in the United States?" I finished.

"He was dragged from the lake yesterday. Does he normally spend, let us see, one day short of three weeks with the patrols?"

"No," I said. "Usually a week or so..."

"Why then did you not report him missing?"

"I just assumed his assignment was for a longer period than..."

"What did he do for you? What did he do here?"

"He cooked, he cleaned."

"You have been here, in business, for years without trouble." I noticed Horacio hadn't touched his coffee, and it was cooling off, had stopped steaming. "I assume you paid him for his services and paid him adequately. Did you owe him money? Or did he owe you?"

"I pay everyone weekly," I said, "on Friday," and I couldn't help but regret the waste that his cooling, useless coffee represented. "We were square when he disappeared."

"Square. Have you spoken with his family?"

"I don't know his family," I said. "I'm not sure he has any." I figured if Carmela, maybe family, maybe not, thought it useful to talk with this man, she would seek him out.

"Did you kill him?"

"No," I said, and though someone else might have been offended, I was not. Whether poets or mechanics or (in those oh so rare instances) both, people aren't necessarily what they appear to be. "He was my friend," I said.

But I *could* have been his killer.

Anybody can be anything.

"So," our chief of police Horacio Quiñones said, "the deceased worked for you for seven years. He was, you claim, your friend. And you are not sure if he has a family?"

"I'm afraid that's correct," I said.

"Hmm."

Anybody can be anything.

CHAPTER XIV
OKIES

Despite Gonzalo's disappearance, I still have had time on my hands, albeit nervous, barren time, and I have remembered that although it was only a couple of days between decision made and decision implemented, I had taken time before Audrey and I left Columbus to contact and talk to all my sisters.

My older sister Rachel, as I've said, lived on the city's north side with her insurance salesman husband Sid and their five kids, including two sets of twins.

"We just can't hack it," I'd told her over the phone the morning after Audrey, finally laughing after our time since Aiken, had asked me so rhetorically, *Is there anything keeping us here, anyone expecting us?*

"It's not so sudden," I told her that afternoon as the three of us, me, Rachel, and Audrey, sat sipping iced tea under the clouds on her redwood deck. Three of her kids were in school. The other two—a boy and a girl whose names, God help me, I still don't remember—were playing in the yard, no more than three feet tall each, tormenting their dog, a red setter named Shane—odd I'd remember that—pulling its furry tail, its floppy ears, giggling when it snapped, barked. "There's not a whole hell of a lot else for us to do," I said.

"What about the hardware store?" Rachel said, then turning toward Audrey, "What about the sewing?" Sid, I believe, had taken the day off to play golf.

"Audrey's folks moved west, you know," I said.

"They seem real happy," Audrey said, looking into her glass. "But they miss me. Us. I'd like to see them."

"Jesus. Just take a vacation," Rachel said, and it seemed she was ready and willing, too much so, to blame Audrey for us leaving town. That wasn't fair, and despite our past I found myself suddenly not liking her for it.

"We'll write," I said, and there must have been a bitterness in my voice. "We'll stay in touch." I could be bitter. The last year or so had given me experience.

Following Horacio Quiñones's visit, this last weekend passed uneventfully, despite Gonzalo's absence. It was the third weekend under such circumstances, after all. I'd had practice.

Festival week was coming up in Sololá, the capital of our state, our *departamento*, called Sololá also. The town sits up the mountain from us toward the Pan-American Highway, toward the road to Guatemala City. Late Sunday evening, after the last of the tourists had gone and Daddy Rabbit's was closed and clean and had been restored to some semblance of order, Nati suggested we both take the day off and go, enjoy ourselves, forget about Gonzalo.

"I don't know," I told her, but of course I did. Since Gonzalo's disappearance, Nati and Carmela had gotten their normal days off, Monday and Tuesday, respectively, but only because I myself had worked without one. There's no way two of us could leave for the day without closing up. I don't like to do that. People expect you to be there. When you aren't, they go somewhere else, taking their money with them. Who knows if they go for good?

And I'd just closed the day they found Gonzalo's body.

Nati looked at me quizzically, waiting, I suppose, for a more definite answer.

I said, "Don't look at me like that. Take your regular day tomorrow. Go ahead and go."

"A *solas*? Alone?"

"You know we can't both go," I said. I mentioned some friends of hers, suggested she look them up.

"I want to be with you."

I could sure sympathize, and I have to admit that for a second I thought about just saying to hell with it, Christ, take the woman. But

I've spent seven years building Daddy Rabbit's' reputation and good will, and I didn't need to be blowing it in the space of a couple of weeks, death in the family or not.

"And I with you," I finally told her, "but no," and when we locked Daddy Rabbit's to head home, she walked quickly ahead of me, her slight hips rocking angrily side to side, walked quickly increasing the distance between us. By the time I reached the alley and turned toward the house she was nowhere to be seen. I feared for a moment that maybe she hadn't gone to the house at all, but had instead fled, I don't know where, to be honest.

Perhaps I don't know Nati all that well either.

She was home when I got there, a crack of light shone above and beneath the bathroom door. I went in to the kitchen, flicked on the overhead light, decided it was too stark and opted instead for the pole lamp beside the back door. I sat down to write, to continue this account, but nothing came out. Instead I made circles on the paper, just doodled, and decided that though I wasn't quite sure how to go about it, I needed to go to work on finding a replacement for Gonzalo. Eventually I heard Nati open the bathroom door, turn out the light, then close what could only be the bedroom door, presumably behind her. In a bit I went up to the bedroom, but the light was out so I didn't enter.

That night I slept, again, down on the couch.

Back to my sisters.

After Audrey and I visited Rachel's but before we left Columbus, I called my sister Linda, still living out in Newark. Neither of us had much to say, it had been so long since we'd really been anything resembling close. Hap wasn't home, out on call refilling twenties in banking machines, I suppose, or it may be that he'd already begun his trips to the prostitutes. Whatever, he almost always answered the phone when I called—Linda, I'm afraid, had gotten a bit lazy—but this time Linda answered, Hap wasn't home.

"What is it?" she said after the formalities were over.

"We're leaving," I said. "Me and Audrey're leaving Columbus."

"Well?" she said, sounding perhaps disinterested, but maybe, I hoped, just preoccupied.

"In a couple of days. Just wanted to say good-bye."

"Bye," she said without expression, and the lack of expression, of concern, hurt. "When are you coming back?"

That explained it. She had misunderstood. "We're not," I said. "At least, as of now, we're not planning to."

"Well," she said.

"We'll call," I said, "or at least write."

"Do that. Have you heard from Hap lately?"

I said I hadn't and that I hoped everything was okay, she said it was, and we concluded our conversation with the same types of formalities with which we had begun it.

The night Audrey and I left Columbus, and in the days that followed, I felt dissatisfied with that good-bye to my sister Linda. It didn't necessarily haunt me, and I eventually got over it, but still. When it comes to family, especially the Hopkins family, you somehow expect to be closer.

Monday here, yesterday now, began much like the Friday before had (and like most days do, of course)—waking up, washing, brushing teeth, dressing—except that when I checked on Nati up in the bed she wasn't there, and then when I opened the door to leave for the restaurant Horacio Quiñones was standing in front of it just getting ready to knock. He was sharply dressed as usual, and flanked on his right, my left, by a man a couple of inches shorter than he, a couple of inches wider as well, hands folded behind his back. He was clearly another policeman of some sort, someone, assuming that the assortment of medals on his chest and lapels were more than mere decoration, the pistol on his hip with its pearl-handled grip something more than a toy, pretty important, high-ranking.

"Señor 'opkins," said Horacio. "May we come in?"

I shrugged my shoulders and stepped back out of their way. I could hardly say no. Horacio entered first, his companion second, stiffly, his hands still behind him. I closed the door.

"This is Colonel Jorge Aguilera Illingworth," Horacio said, and I immediately recognized the name, the unforgettable last name so clearly not native. Aguilera Illingworth was one of the military commissioners of *el departamento* of Sololá. And, despite my attempts over the years to ignore, or at least avoid, Guatemalan politics, I was aware of his reputation as a man ruthless in his torture of suspected rebels. It was impossible not to be. The local Indians spoke of him as much as of anyone, and always with a combination of fear and hatred. Horacio continued: "He would like to ask you a few questions concerning the death of your employee Gonzalo Méndez Paredes."

"Have you dug up anything new?"

"Please," Horacio said, "let the Colonel ask the questions."

I was more than willing to, though as I said it didn't seem I really had a choice in the matter, and I didn't at all like this continuing feeling that I myself might be a suspect. Aguilera Illingworth didn't seem to be all that anxious to begin asking, either. He had walked to the front corner and was leaning over, hands still clasped behind his back, inspecting the two waist-high plants, a schefflera and a ficus of some sort—Nati knows the plants better than I do—that sat beneath the two corner windows. He suddenly stood, wheeled around, and said something quickly and brusquely in Spanish to Horacio. When he finished speaking he unclasped his hands and moved the right one to his mouth and began chewing on its thumbnail.

"He wants to know if you are going to water your plants," said Horacio, still standing near the door.

"Tell him they're due," I said. "Tell him I'll water them as soon as he leaves." And he can leave any time, I thought, but of course I didn't say that.

Horacio turned to Aguilera Illingworth and spoke, translating, I assume, though my Spanish is still so poor I have no way of knowing. I would simply have to trust him, this man who had been so unassuming and invisible to me for the last seven years, so much so that I had no idea whether I could in fact trust him or not.

The colonel glanced at me ever so briefly then returned his attention to Horacio. He spoke again, same tone as before.

"He asks that you tell him all you know of the death of Gonzalo Méndez Paredes," Horacio said.

"Tell him nothing," I said, and realized I might be mis-phrasing that. "No," I said, "tell him I would gladly tell him all I know, but I don't

124

know anything. I don't. I was hoping the two of you could tell me."

Horacio spoke again to Aguilera Illingworth, translating. Or not. The two began a conversation between themselves, Horacio still by the door, the colonel still in the corner, hands behind him when he was speaking, thumbnail in his mouth when he was listening. Each man glanced my way only here and there. I might as well have been a schefflera or a ficus myself. Finally I moved slowly, leisurely—no telling what reaction sudden moves might bring—toward the stairs to the upper level, thinking briefly about sitting in one of the chairs on either side of them. I decided to stand, however. To make these two men, or at least the colonel, look up to me instead of the other way around. I leaned back against the hip-high bannister, folded my arms across my chest, and at some point Horacio addressed me again:

"I am not certain he believes you, Señor 'opkins." He frowned. "I am not certain I do, either."

"Are you going to arrest me, Señor Quiñones?"

"Are you suggesting that we should, sir?"

"I'm only wondering," I said. "Did you come here to arrest me?" Christ, how would Audrey's Nero Wolfe be handling this? Or even my mother and father's Robert Mitchum in that movie from their first date? No help. I hadn't read the books or listened much when Audrey told me of them, but I'd seen that movie, and still no help. I hadn't paid close enough attention.

Quiñones and Aguilera Illingworth were once more carrying on their own private conversation.

"Did you come here to arrest me?" I repeated, interrupting, trying, unsuccessfully I'm sure, not to let my voice show my agitation. Or my fear, either. They continued speaking as though I weren't in the room, till finally Horacio again spoke in my direction:

"In answer to your question, we came here only to find out what you might know about the death of your friend and employee. However, because of what he terms the evasive nature of your answers, Colonel Aguilera Illingworth is considering holding you—arresting you, if that is the wording on which you insist—as a material witness. First, though, he would like to know if you own a gun."

This was too much.

"Of course I don't own a goddamned gun!" I yelled. What grave was I digging now? "And I'm not a witness, material or otherwise. I own my house and some furniture, what you see..."

The colonel shot a frown towards Horacio, and though Horacio was looking at me he must have caught it out of the corner of his eye.

"You do not have to yell, *Señor* 'opkins," he said, "and you would do well not to."

"Well, Christ, Quiñones, I own a little restaurant, a little bar. I may not have been born here, but I'm a citizen now, my papers are all in order."

For better or worse, I was on a roll, so I continued:

"I pay taxes. I support tourism. And I don't fucking shoot people, especially my friends! And you and your goddamned colonel can both go to hell."

I was breathing rapidly, my chest heaving, almost to the point of hyperventilating. I suddenly noticed that without realizing it I had moved off the bannister and backed up a couple of the stairs. I also saw that Aguilera Illingworth had his right hand on the pistol on his hip, his left at the ready to unsnap its holster. I figured it might be time to sit down, so I did. The colonel eased his hands back behind him.

"I'm sorry," I said. "But I can't help you. Gonzalo worked for me for seven years, and was probably my best friend in Tela. But I didn't know his family, I didn't know what he did or where he went when he wasn't working. If the colonel here is involved, then his death must have something to do with the rebels, but if Gonzalo was one himself I have no idea. He built my roof. He cooked. He cleaned. He translated for me. We drank a beer together now and then, but when we talked we only talked about the business, about Daddy Rabbit's. About little things." I looked to the colonel. His eyes were black, small, unfriendly, unyielding. "Find who killed him," I said to him, or more precisely said at him. He didn't understand, as far as I knew. "He was my best friend."

I sat on the stairs, my elbows resting on my knees, my breathing slowing little by little. Quiñones and the colonel were back in private conversation, and though I could only catch a word here and there, I sensed that they weren't going to arrest me after all (though I can't say for certain that they never intended to). Finally they made signs to leave.

"The Colonel says you should take better care of your plants," said Horacio, and he took a step toward me to allow Colonel Jorge Aguilera Illingworth, military commissioner of the Guatemalan *departamento* of Sololá, to exit first.

"I will," I said, feeling relieved, of course, but perhaps broken somewhat, too, like a wild horse, a mustang, they likely called them in Arizona, though I've never thought of myself as wild, as someone so impertinent and independent as to need breaking.

Horacio leaned his head toward me, me still sitting on the stairs, and said in a whisper, "One thing before I go, *Señor* 'opkins."

"Yes."

"I have a nephew," he said. "My wife's sister's son. His name is Edelberto, Edelberto Morales Arroyave."

"Yes?" I said.

"He is good with his hands. His father, my *cuñado*, is a carpenter across the lake. Perhaps you know of him."

"Hmm," I said.

"And like me he is good with English."

"Can the boy cook?"

"He is a smart one, the smartest of my sister's sons. He can learn."

I told Horacio to have him come by Daddy Rabbit's early Wednesday morning then thanked him for his help, in finding someone to replace Gonzalo, in dealing with the colonel. No matter, I suppose, that in either case or in both how he conducted himself had much more to do with his own interest than with mine.

That's fine. People do what they have to do. I know.

Sister number three:

Audrey and I had dropped by my sister Jane's the same night we'd gone to Rachel's, but she wasn't home. Too bad. I would've liked to see her.

I called her instead, the night before Audrey and I left Columbus. We talked for a while, I filled her in on our plans, such as they were, she told me she'd miss us. Then finally, "Write," she said so cheerfully as the conversation was winding down. She was in her fourth year at Ohio State then, still studying poetry, still living with Stevie's sister Christine.

Despite her childhood, she seemed as a young adult to be the happiest of us. I liked that. "Be sure to write," she said. And though it sounded more like an assignment, or maybe like an admonition from one of her poetry teachers than something you might say to your only brother as he was leaving town, speaking with you maybe for the last time ever, I said I would.

And of course, I have.

It may be that what I'm writing now is as much to her as to anybody.

Writing.

My one-armed grandfather Tom Hopkins, more than half a century ago, had something to say in his section of the journals about writing as well as about the type of traveling, the migration, you might call it, that Audrey and I undertook as we left Columbus—no, Aiken, then Columbus—and my sisters:

> *July 28, 1938*
>
> *First entry in months. For all who someday may read this, most of all to young Tom, I apologize. The responsibility for this writing is a real one and should be taken seriously.*
>
> *Life goes on here, same now as ever. Day upon day, though, news comes of people in other parts of the country moving to still other parts. Oklahoma comes to mind, in what they've been calling the "Dust Bowl."*
>
> *Sounds like people are hurting out that way. I wonder, though, if they might not be better off waiting it out, waiting for times to turn in their favor. The way life goes in cycles, it's bound to come back for them. The grass is rarely greener on the other side of the hill.*
>
> *I suppose it's likely they have waited, though. One part of the country to another, despite a few people who just follow the latest fashion to be following, most folks are as sensible as not. If the Okies have decided to head west, most of them probably know damned well it's their best, or only, option.*
>
> *God forbid the same should ever happen here.*
>
> *I promise now to record whatever observations I may have more*

often. This is a solemn pledge.

Thomas Nelson Hopkins II

Earlier I said that the Depression must not have affected Aiken much. Well, strike that. It could just be that it hit us late, like fifty years or so. Audrey and I, fleeing that dying town, fleeing the fading remnants of what was once the fulfillment of my ancestors' dreams, then a year or so later leaving Columbus and its hopelessness, we may have been little different from those desperate Oklahoma farmers. We may have simply been modern-day Okies.

The visit from Quiñones and Aguilera Illingworth came yesterday morning, Monday morning. After my visitors left I went to the restaurant, where I found Carmela working, of course, still red-eyed, puffy, but increasingly coming back to life: by mid-afternoon she had energetically, loudly chased two stray dogs from the kitchen, three cats from the dining area.

Nati was there too, working on her day off, apologetic, warm, affectionate. I didn't know what to make of that, still don't. If I had the space of a book in which to characterize our relationship, I couldn't do it. Its nuances baffle me.

I closed the restaurant today, Tuesday. Who could explain that, after my thoughts on it the day before? It may be that the events of Monday morning suggested to me that life, particularly my life, may be, *seriously* may be, too short to have its turns dictated by worries about tomorrow's business. Whatever, this morning Nati and I took a bus up the hill to visit the *festival* in Sololá. Ate, drank wine, hugged and kissed each other maybe a little too much, celebrated nothing more than summer. We returned to Tela before dark, made love on the floor of the front room— we do make love now and then—again up in the bed. It was good.

She's sleeping now. Again I'm alone, writing, writing something that somehow seems more important the deeper I get into it, more worthy of inclusion in the Hopkins family journals, more a necessary part of them. Maybe I'm finally beginning to understand exactly what they are, exactly what their existence represents.

And maybe not.

At this moment I can hear the jeeps and the personnel carriers that bring the civil patrols into Tela rattling, rumbling by on the streets outside, the boys shouting, laughing. They're coming to protect us, I suppose, but protect us from what? From rebels? From cooks, from carpenters?

From themselves?

From the CIA, maybe, maybe from one son-of-a-bitch colonel or another.

Thank you, boys, and may God or somebody be with you.

The death of Gonzalo Méndez Paredes is a mystery, and clearly just one among many which I'm ill-equipped to solve. I don't have A SNOW-BALL'S CHANCE IN HELL, as Grandpa Tom might put it, of finding Gonzalo's killer, of figuring out damn near anything.

Chapter XV
The First Daddy Rabbit's

Audrey and I spent a month and a half living out of the truck, camping in state parks for minimal fees, eating fruits and vegetables and lunchmeats from local mom-and-pops, washing up in streams or occasional park showers. Being frugal with my dead father's money, we saw Indiana, Illinois, Missouri, Arkansas, Mississippi and Louisiana. Texas, Oklahoma, Kansas. Finally, we reached Colorado and Denver, and it, more so than everywhere we'd been and everywhere we'd come from— lovely Aiken, the other places in Ohio—seemed someplace historic, a place important. As we drove in we thought, or at least I did, maybe here's somewhere we can stay, make a home, begin life again.

Oh, well.

YOU CAN'T JUDGE A BOOK BY ITS COVER.

We quickly got hired to manage that apartment building on Corona I mentioned earlier, the Huntington (1892 engraved on the granite transom), and a first-floor apartment came with it, utilities paid.

A young couple lived on the top floor, two floors directly above us. A Friday night in December, some time long after Audrey and I had gone to bed, we were awakened by someone knocking on our door. It was a frantic-type of knocking, rapid-fire, agitated. No telling how long it had gone on before we answered.

Audrey reached it first, and by the time I got out to the front room the girl from that apartment two floors above us was sitting at our kitchen table, wearing my flatblack thrift store raincoat and, Audrey told me later, nothing more. The color and lusterless sheen of the coat matched her hair.

"He's nothing but a cocksucker," she was yelling, her voice hoarse, her right hand shaking so much that as she lifted a cigarette to her mouth she at first missed. "That's what he was when I met him, that's what he is now." She couldn't have been more than twenty, still had baby fat in her cheeks, neck, thighs. "A whore, just a little boy whore." Audrey took the cigarette from her, the matches too (a crimson pack, the first Daddy Rabbit's logo in silver script). She lit the cigarette then placed it between the girl's lips. Where had she learned to do that? No one in her family had smoked, or, as I've said, in mine either.

Maybe my secrets wouldn't be the only ones between us. The girl continued:

"A little boy whore cocksucking his way around Colorado Springs." I noticed that the skin around her left eye was turning purple, becoming a pretty good shiner. She was beginning to shiver, too. I had been standing in the kitchen doorway, my plaid flannel robe wrapped around me, no belt holding it, just my hands. I wasn't cold. Audrey always slept in those days in a cotton nightgown, low-cut but ankle-length, and that's what she was wearing then.

"Are you cold, Audrey?" I asked her.

She shook her head.

"You?" I said at the girl in my raincoat, whose name, I realized, I didn't know.

She gave me a puzzled look, and I had to figure her shiver was over something else. Shock, maybe. Maybe drugs. Who knew? Not me.

As usual, whatever the hell was going on was somehow beyond me. I smiled at Audrey and the girl, hoping my expression to be one, respectively, supporting and comforting. That's all I could do, I figured. Then I went to bed. Audrey, as she did with most of the apartment-related business but for the boiler, took care of the situation. I had to get to sleep. I had to be at work early in the morning.

Audrey called the police. I guess the kid the girl lived with had beat her pretty good, given her bruises I hadn't seen beneath my coat, even broken a finger. The police came, left. They took the girl with them, who knew where. I slept.

Another evening, so much more recent, no less eventful:

Despite the nightly presence in Tela of the *patrullas civiles*, the civil patrols, despite the bombing before my arrival of the Hotel Tela, despite Gonzalo's recent disappearance and death, most of the guerrilla activity in our area took place more than seven or eight years ago. The sound of gunfire around here then is something very rare. Wednesday evening, though, just about the time the civil patrols normally roll into town and down the *Avenida* Santander in their American Jeeps and their Ford F-500s, we heard it, me and Nati, *saw* it, in fact, the blue-white flashes accompanying the tiny explosions as we sat in my house eating dinner, as we saw the wood of the walls beside us suddenly split and reveal fresh white wood, then looked quickly to each other as if that would somehow verify what we'd seen.

We scrambled to the floor, saying nothing, not yelling or screaming, hit it both of us at the same time, waited, grabbed each other's hands beneath the table, squeezed tightly. Waited some more.

Nothing.

More.

Nothing.

I heard the grating sputter of the patrols' vehicles rise then fade, that chatter of its occupants, that laughter, all now irritating, maddening.

Hijueputas.

You'll have to figure out for yourself how that translates, what it means.

When I was reasonably certain the patrols, and thus the danger, had passed, I let go of Nati's hand, and we stood up. I went to the wall behind the table, touched my fingers to the splintered wood where the bullets—there appeared to have been two—struck. With my eyes I searched the room, noticed another gouged spot on the bannister, a third bullet. When I turned back to the table, Nati was seated, calmly and quietly finishing her dessert, her mango. Yes, though it must have been some time back, she'd seen this before, lived through it. Just a return to old routine. I wished I had her courage, if that's what it was. I was afraid.

I went to the front windows, the corner ones with the schefflera and the ficus beneath them. In the streets, the streets always dark at night, I could see nothing. A gentle rain mimicking the one earlier in the afternoon was just beginning. I couldn't hear the patrols anymore. Presumably they were down at the lake, likely raiding the restaurants down there for free fish and beer.

I had assumed at first that the gunfire had come from them, the patrols. Now suddenly I wasn't so sure, though if it had come from someone else certainly they would have responded with some of their own. Unless, of course, they had received instructions not to, orders to ignore whatever might happen in the vicinity of *la casa del norteamericano*, of my house.

Knowing I could do nothing about the shooting, especially tonight, I closed and latched the front window, then the side one, then the rest of the windows on the lower level. I rejoined Nati, and after dinner, after cleaning up afterwards, we slept together, close together, held each other tightly.

I worked at a liquor store in Denver, Singer Spirits, a couple of blocks away from the Huntington up on Colfax. As with my earlier job working for Gary Gombos at Davidson Hardware, I found it through the obituaries. I got hired as a replacement for a dead assistant manager by the Singer brothers themselves within a couple of weeks of our move into the Huntington. I won't bore you with the details. I'll only say that the job came so easy that for weeks I worried I might be, as my grandfather Tom might have put it, RESTING ON MY LAURELS, that it came too easy. There must be some catch.

But there wasn't any catch as far I could figure. My primary job was to receive wine and liquor orders, and within a couple of months I knew enough about the business and had earned enough of the brothers' trust to place the orders myself. Pay was good enough that Audrey didn't have to rush out looking for work herself. And I was able to bank the rest of my father's thousands, still most of what we'd started out with back when he'd died.

In December, the call came from my sister Rachel that Grandpa Herman, in Cincinnati then, had passed away. A "sudden heart attack," she said, as if there were some other kind. As I said earlier, Audrey and I went by train to the funeral. We left Tuesday afternoon from Union

Station, had a short layover in Chicago, then reached Cincinnati early Thursday morning. At the funeral I got to see all three of my sisters—they had driven down together, without their two husbands and one girl-friend. We kissed, hugged, cried a bit. At least we must have. I really don't remember the details. I had had a couple of drinks on the train and wasn't altogether with it, and within a couple of hours after the burial Audrey and I were back on the train for the return trip.

We got back on a Saturday. The Huntington was still standing. Monday I'd be back at work. The trip marked the last time I saw Ohio, the last time I saw my sisters, and it set us back $648.38, plus food and drinks. It must have been worth it.

Worth surprises one; comparative worth surprises even more.

Last Wednesday morning, Edelberto Morales Arroyave, Horacio Quiñones's nephew from across the lake, had showed up at Daddy Rabbit's just before noon, before lunch. I was sitting at my usual table just inside the door tending to business, deciding how much, if anything, closing the doors the day before might have cost me. Nothing, I was finding out, not sure what that meant.

"*Señor* 'opkins," a voice said quietly, and I looked up. "My Uncle Horacio sent me." The man was tall, taller than Quiñones, and, I realized when I stood up to shake his hand, taller than me, standing at least a couple of inches over six feet. Very unusual. His square face, appearing wider than it was long, hinted at Indian, but with his height I figured he must have even more *ladino* blood than his uncle. He wore a white work shirt, open at the collar, blue work pants covered waist to knee by a native wraparound, vertical stripes in five or six colors, and black leather sandals, no socks. Nothing unusual there.

"*Bienvenidos*," I said. "*Mucho gusto*. I'm glad you could come." His face seemed slightly scarred, though not from acne, maybe from fire, maybe not at all. Whatever it was it gave him the look of a man older than I'd expected. No matter. I needed someone. "Your uncle says you know English."

"I speak it as if it were my own tongue," he said proudly and indeed with barely a trace of an accent. I motioned for him to sit, and he did, placing one hand in his lap, the other on the table. I returned to my chair.

"And your father's a carpenter," I continued. "Are you good with your hands too?"

"I am not a carpenter, *Señor* 'opkins, but I am the best of mechanics."

A mechanic, not a poet. A worker, not a ponderer.

He glanced back quickly over his shoulder, then turned his eyes back to me. "I work on cars, and trucks, and motors. I build them and I repair them. I also can learn what you need for me to learn. I am certain of that."

"Good," I said, believing him, and I noticed something in his eyes that hinted he might be just a boy after all. It wasn't an innocence—no one in Guatemala, especially here in the highlands, is innocent, no one but tourists. It was that the skin around his eyes sat smooth, not wrinkled like the rest of his face, his neck. Yes, that was it. "You speak well," I said. "I don't speak Spanish worth a damn. Can you translate?"

"At times I have worked in such a capacity."

"For who?"

"For tourists, of course." He glanced over his shoulder, then back. "And for one official or another."

Though he came from just the other side of the lake, that portion of the other side happened to lie in a different *departamento*, Chimaltenango. I wondered if he might be associated with its military, with its police, figuring he very well could be—take his Uncle Horacio, for example. From across the lake whoever he might know wouldn't have any business, or jurisdiction, in Tela though. I had no reason to worry, so I didn't ask about it. I asked instead if he could cook, he said he certainly could, when growing up he wasn't at his Uncle Danilo's knee at the shop he was at his aunts' and his mother's in their kitchen, and I said fine, but I said nothing else. Carmela could be a better judge of his abilities and his eventual worth than I.

"If you work for me here," I asked, "will you have a place to live?" I'm not sure why I wanted to know. Maybe I just wanted him to understand that I was in the market for a permanent replacement for Gonzalo, not a temporary, transient one.

"My uncle Horacio says I may live with him and *mi tía* Claribel," he answered. "He has a room, he says, where I may stay without intruding."

I meant to be smiling at him, at this tall, thin, this very polite and likable young Edelberto Morales Arroyave. Apparently I was frowning instead. Who knows what I might have been thinking.

"Is that not acceptable?" he said.

"No, sir. I mean yes, of course it is. Should I call you Edelberto?"

He said that would be fine, that's what his friends call him, that or simply Bert.

"Well?" I said. "Bert? Or Edelberto? Which will it be?"

"As I said, sir, either one. I answer gladly to both."

I said I would call him Edelberto till I knew him better, then I took him back to the kitchen to work for awhile with Carmela. She greeted him with her usual gruffness, but she also told me just after lunch that Wednesday, with little more than a nod of her head and a few hand signals, that if an occasional cook was what I was looking for, then this young man Edelberto would do fine. He would earn his pay. Through early afternoon, he and I talked job description. He would cook, clean, maintain the premises, make himself available for occasional translation. We talked salary—forty *quetzales* a week to start, ten less than Gonzalo but I didn't know him yet, plus leftovers if and when he wanted them.

He would begin Thursday morning. Which is now this morning. As I always do, I'm writing at my house. If all is going well, Gonzalo's replacement is already down at Daddy Rabbit's, following Carmela's instructions about cooking, cleaning.

Christ, I hope he's not a spy.

Not that I have anything to hide.

Back to Denver. Sometime in January. A mostly cold month there but a month in which a sunny, seventy-degree day could show up and surprise you, I began to visit the first Daddy Rabbit's, Daddy Rabbit's Lounge, Topless Dancers. The first visit was innocent enough, and I told Audrey about it.

Sammy Singer was the younger of my two bosses, but he was still several years older than I. He was a good forty, fifty pounds overweight, he perspired constantly and sloppily, and one tapered flap of his dress shirt always hung out of his pants. He was married as well, to an attractive, well-kept woman who couldn't have weighed more than ninety pounds.

Sammy was lucky to have her. Unless, of course, she wasn't the fine (though thin) catch she appeared to be. It didn't seem right that he should visit the strip joints.

Of course, it didn't seem right that I should either, being so lucky to be married to Audrey.

But I did.

One bright Wednesday afternoon in January Sammy suggested we go. Just have a drink, take the day's edge off. Out of a sense of obligation—when you work for someone else, you become accustomed to doing what the boss says—but out of curiosity too, I guess, I went.

Inside was dark. White bulbs outlined the dancers' runway and stage, the mirrors behind the bars that ran lengthwise down either side of the room. Speakers above the stage and at the room's far end blared and pounded with thick, squealing guitars and drums, cried with a singer's screeching falsetto. A mixture of aromas assaulted and surrounded us, musky and floral perfumes and colognes, the yeast of beer, the sharpness of alcohol. We took a table near the stage, though where we sat didn't seem as if it should make a difference—in all directions women naked from the waist up, in their G-strings practically so from the waist down, served drinks, danced and pranced smooth-skinned and brown-skinned around and on top of tables, stuck their breasts, crotches, and butts into the customers' laps and faces.

To say I'd never seen anything like it would certainly be an understatement.

Recall Aiken, for example, and the Christmas cantata that finally brought Audrey and me together. Recall, in fact, anything about Aiken at all.

I drank bourbon and water, then simply straight bourbon, what had been my father's drink. Sammy yelled loudly, rudely, and a lot. Eventually I did too, at first embarrassed, later not.

That day one of the dancers, bleached blonde, heavier than most of the others though not at all fat, danced at our table. It cost a few extra bucks, but Sammy willingly paid. Earlier the DJ had introduced her as "Dallas"—others went by names like Star, April, Misty, Rain—so that's what we called her. At one point she placed her hands warmly on my knees and leaned forward, letting her breasts, breasts in their fullness the opposite of Audrey's, swing a couple of inches from my face. Then she leaned down and whispered in my ear, in a husky voice:

"You'd be handsome if you smiled more."

I hadn't been smiling, had been consciously avoiding it, of course I didn't know how to act in such a place, if smiling at the dancers was rude, if it would make me look like the jerk Sammy had at first seemed to be.

This Dallas leaned back, tilted her head to one side, and looked at my mouth. I smiled then. Had to. "That's better," she said, then she came forward again and blew on my neck, hot breath, breath that would give a guy a hard on right now. It did, and that's all it took. I was hooked.

As I said, I told Audrey about that visit, explaining it as a one-time thing forced upon me by Sammy Singer.

"Sammy Singer's a creep," Audrey said. "I hope this isn't a sign of things to come." And though it was, neither of us knew it at the time, so we laughed about it.

I hadn't told her, though, about Dallas. Neither, in the months to come, did I tell her about any of the other dozen or so visits I made to Daddy Rabbit's, about the words I whispered to the woman I foolishly came to think of as my Dallas or to some dancer or another, about the closeness I felt with any of them, with their skin, their smells, their sex. As I said earlier, though, it wouldn't surprise me if Audrey knew. But certainly she had her own secrets, so while I felt somewhat guilty about it all, I was able to rationalize some of that guilt away.

I'm not sure how I feel about it today, if I'm ashamed or not. I guess I'll have to leave that kind of judgment to someone else. To whoever might read this, for example, whether it becomes part of the journals or not.

Spring came to Denver, and though we didn't speak to each other of it, again restlessness took hold of me and Audrey. Who could say why? Could it be simply that, comfortable as we'd become, we still weren't home? No family nearby, no roots?

Whatever, we left Denver and Singer Spirits and the Huntington (and the first Daddy Rabbit's) to work at the Flying Z Ranch a couple of hundred miles north, in Wyoming. The move came suddenly, Audrey reading casually through the Sunday classifieds of the *Post*, showing me the ad, me saying, "Why not?" and the two of us taking the truck up to apply that same day. We were hired and moved up the first of June, 1984, a year after we'd left Columbus, two after we'd left Aiken.

I was glad to leave the girls of the first Daddy Rabbit's behind. You can only keep a secret like that so long. Better to QUIT WHILE YOU'RE AHEAD, even if it takes a move of you, your wife, and everything you owned to another state to force you to.

Thoughts puzzle. After Edelberto left yesterday afternoon, and before the dinner hour was to begin, I had some time to think about Gonzalo's murder, maybe about the nature of murder in general, at least about the murderer. If I were to discover his identity, or hers, I figured, nursing a light Gallo, still sitting at my corner table, I would have to consider three angles: means, opportunity, and motive. Still, such a method could only allow me to eliminate one person or another—myself included—not to conclusively deduce who may be the guilty party.

For example, I could look at myself as a possible suspect. Gonzalo was killed by gunshot, assuming the hole in his forehead as the cause of death, a safe assumption but by no means a certain one. I don't have a gun, I don't have access to one, I've never fired one in my life. Thus, I didn't have the *means* to murder my friend Gonzalo.

Now, I certainly had the opportunity to kill him. Recall that his body was found some two weeks or so after he first came up missing from Daddy Rabbit's. If he spent the first week of that time doing his duty with the civil patrols, then he may have been missing for only a week, the second of the two. Still, though, barring some forensic method of which I'm not aware (and there's no reason I should be) there might be no way, especially in a place as likely forensically backward as Tela, to place time of death any more precisely than sometime during those two weeks. Add to that the fact that although Gonzalo was found floating in the lake, he may or may not have died in it, or even in its vicinity. So yes, I had the *opportunity* to kill Gonzalo. But, I had to figure, so did just about everyone else in the country. Without time and place of death, there could be no alibis, for almost anyone.

That brought me to the subject of motive. I had none. He didn't owe me money, nor I him. We weren't vying for the affections of the same woman—I had Nati, he had, who knows? I have no secrets here that he may have discovered, secrets that if revealed would embarrass me or expose me to legal action or ruin my business. We'd never fought, never even argued, too much respect for each other, I guess. And if I had killed him, it wasn't an act done in the heat of passion. I don't have that much passion these days, of course I never have.

So I had no *motive* to kill him, nor did I have the means. Like just about everyone else, however, I had the opportunity. One out of three's not enough, though. Clearly I didn't do it, I could eliminate myself, but that only brought me slightly closer to finding out who killed him, if it did even that.

This might be a slow process, I had to figure.

It couldn't have been later than three o'clock or so, but through the restaurant's front windows I noticed that the streets appeared quite dark. The afternoon thunder clouds typical of mid-summer around the lake must have begun to form. I saw just Carmela's round head through the window, moving in the direction of the lake down *Avenida* Santander. She often took a break mid-afternoon, visited the market or some other shop or restaurant, friends. She must have felt comfortable enough with our new Edelberto Morales Arroyave to leave him on his own for a while. I checked on him back in the kitchen anyway.

As boss I have to do something.

He was scrubbing some dishes, and he nodded at me and smiled. I returned his smile, went behind the bar where Nati was working, kissed her quickly on her soft cheek, got myself a second beer, and returned to my table. Time to consider other suspects.

I did so, mostly fishing, just mentally fishing, night-fishing blind. Means, I narrowed down to *la policia*, Horacio Quiñones and Colonel Jorge Aguilera Illingworth included; to the men who served in *las patrulles civiles*, but only when they, whoever they were, were on duty— most wouldn't have guns in their possession otherwise. Still, whoever they were, they were too numerous to consider. And to, of course, my part-time neighbor and sometimes friend Miguel Romero, a.k.a. Michael Roberts of Chicago, Illinois. He had guns, rifles and shotguns in that rack in the hallway, and handguns I'd never seen close up, only lying on a desk or a table in the distance. From his spy days, he'd always said, leftovers. But now, who knew?

I briefly considered Gonzalo himself as having the means, considered that his death may after all have been simple suicide. But the police, at least Quiñones and Aguilera Illingworth, hadn't seemed to think so. Why should I? I considered suicide as a possibility, then quickly discarded it. Outside a light rain began, then just as quickly ended.

Opportunity, again, was a wash. Everybody had it.

Motive? I knew no one who hadn't liked my friend and employee Gonzalo Méndez Paredes, no one who may have carried a grudge against him, no one, in short, who may have wished him dead. Of course, as my interview with Quiñones and Aguilera Illingworth had most recently demonstrated, there was much about Gonzalo, especially about his personal doings, I didn't know. Had he been, in secret, a rebel, even a rebel leader? Someone whose activities made him ripe for disappearance?

I supposed he could have been, one or the other or both, though I'd never seen sign of anything such. Again, Gonzalo was foremost, in Proctor's scheme, a mechanic rather than a poet. Or at least he appeared to be. Foremost a doer, not a thinker. A follower, and though not necessarily a leader, possibly a planner.

Again though, despite what the official line might be, we don't appear to have rebels around Tela and this shore of Lake Atitlán, no specific activity that can be attributed to them for years. If Gonzalo was a rebel, he was a dumb one, out of place and out of time.

But if he wasn't a rebel, wasn't affiliated with them at any time or in any manner, then what? Had he seen something he wasn't supposed to see, and then been seen seeing?

Maybe, but yesterday afternoon I couldn't imagine what, and finally I put the matter away.

The only incident that kept nagging at me had come unbidden, and was something I'd ignored at first—Miguel's strange behavior the day of the discovery of the body. Still, through dinner I smiled at my customers, congregated with them, drank with them, though not too much, laughed with them and even posed for a photograph here and there. BUSINESS AS USUAL.

Then we all closed up—young Edelberto Morales Arroyave mopped back then front to finish—Nati and I went home and had dinner, and during dessert and before we slept so closely with each other the shooting began. I didn't know what to make of it, but, I supposed, it was time I must.

It was time I paid Miguel Romero, a.k.a. Michael Roberts of Chicago, Illinois, invisible since the day of the discovery of Gonzalo's body, the day of his own strange behavior, a visit.

CHAPTER XVI
BULL

An acquaintance of mine who runs a jewelry shop up across from the produce market owns a car, an old Mexican Ford. He's offered to let me borrow it from time to time, to go up to market at Chichicastenango, to visit the Mayan ruins in Tikal or the old Spanish capital Antigua, to head into Guatemala City and take in some culture for a change—he eats at Daddy Rabbit's once or twice a week, and it may be that he would like me to visit the city to see how a *real* restaurant prepares food. I'd never taken him up on his offer, but by about mid-morning Friday, nearly a week ago now, I thought it might be time to do so.

After I made the decision to look up Miguel Romero, to discover exactly what he knew about Gonzalo's death, I first walked up to the restaurant to let the others know, Carmela, the new Edelberto, and of course lovely and brave Nati, that I might not be around for lunch.

Nati was out among the tables, cleaning up, replacing the flowers in their vases, and as I saw her something suddenly occurred to me that inexplicably hadn't before.

As far as I knew, *I* was the only one of the three of us who had worked with Gonzalo that the police had questioned.

"Nati," I said. It was nice to see her.

She looked up, smiled, then said softly, "*Buenos días, mi* Jerry."

Of course I again melted, then said that I knew we hadn't talked about it, but had the police spoken with her about Gonzalo, about who might have killed him?

"*Claro que no*," she said, of course not, "I would have told you."

"I know," I said. "Just making certain." I made to go to the kitchen, but before I reached the door, Nati spoke again:

"No, Jerry," she said. "*No han hablado a* Carmela, either."

And with that, I told Nati what I came to tell her, that I might not be around for lunch. I asked her how Edelberto was doing, she said something akin to fine, just fine, both she and Carmela liked him, he worked well. I returned home, waited a few nervous minutes for who knew what, just stalling, I guess, then went and knocked on Miguel's door. His housekeeper, an Indian woman old enough to be Nati's grandmother, Carmela's mother, informed me that he indeed hadn't been home for days, he had gone to his country *villa*, hadn't said when he might return. I had been to that house only once, years ago, but still figured that if I had any sense at all I should be able to find it. Within the hour I found myself wrestling with the clutch and the gear shift of my jeweler acquaintance's Mexican Ford—it was the first time I'd been behind the wheel in seven years—and managing passably well, crossing the *Calle Laguna* bridge over the slim *Río Tela*, headed south, more or less, out of town, the direction I remembered the house lying.

The Flying Z Ranch in southeastern Wyoming, characterized as it was by its desolateness and its isolation, when Audrey and I arrived in June of '84 seemed more like home to us than anywhere else we'd lived over the previous couple of years. More, in its apparent nothingness, like tiny and at the time at least two years dead Aiken, Ohio. It made no pretense of being a community.

So when in early September we left the Flying Z, both me and Audrey wished we could have stayed longer. We had been interviewed, then hired, by Scott and Susan Geller. They were new themselves as ranch managers, brought on board by owner Henry Chilcutt himself only a couple of weeks earlier, and we liked them very much. The two were in their forties, old ranch hands born and bred in and around the barren country of the Sand Hills of Nebraska, but each with a degree in range management from Colorado State University down in Fort Collins.

Scott stood an inch or so shorter than I, was thin and angular top to bottom, crew cut beneath his gray Stetson, clean shaven. He spoke, his voice thin like his more physical features, and his black bolo tie bobbed following his Adam's apple:

"If you can start next week," he said to us at the end of our interview, "we can sure enough use you."

"I think we can do that," Audrey said, speaking for both of us, "I think we'd like it," her cool, even voice a stunning contrast to his.

He coughed, handed his cigarette to his wife Susan, who quickly took a full draw herself. "Then come on up," he said. "Plan on movin' in to that double wide back by the junk yard, then, and I'll be looking for something for you all to do, some work to get you all started. Ain't no use pissin' around."

I nodded silently, which seemed appropriate. I noticed Audrey was smiling, not in laughter, not mocking, but comfortable. That was good.

She thanked Scott, seemed to fall over herself doing it, a woman I wasn't sure I knew, then walked off hand in hand with his wife Susan. Scott and I spoke for a while. I don't recall what about. By that time in our marriage, Audrey was doing all the important talking for both of us.

Scott's wife Susan was a small woman, very small, shorter and thinner than Audrey. She wore her silver hair, hair dyed silver, in a beehive, which on her and next to Scott didn't look as strange or as anachronistic as you might imagine. As she and Audrey walked off after our interview toward some barn-like building, a building which a week or so later we would find out housed stalls, tack, and hay for the Chilcutts' few horses, a goat whose function it was to provide milk for Boss Henry Chilcutt's large daughter Robin, who it turned out was allergic somehow to regular cow's milk, I noticed that small, very-slim Susan had an extremely round, appealing bottom, made more so by the places her jeans had faded to white, the places most round and hand-sized. Thinking of the women of Denver's Daddy Rabbit's—and it didn't take much effort, I had just seen them the day before—I hoped it wouldn't become a problem for me.

It didn't, then or later. Maybe there was something about that hair-do after all.

Heading south, more or less, out of Tela, my borrowed car was the only car on the road. Traffic on weekdays, even in the summer, stays sparse. I stopped on the bridge, shifted into neutral, let the car idle for a moment. Without the kind of shade-tree cover found in town, the hillsides, the terraced farms, the rows above rows of short, gnarled coffee trees were all visible without obstruction. Our country, its countryside, was really quite beautiful. A deep green such as Aiken, Ohio, never saw, a mist present even on a warm summer morning like this one, a white mist softening outlines, confusing and distorting, though somehow comfortingly, all sense of depth.

The car idled quietly, with intermittent sputtering, the exhaust only slightly pungent, barely noticeable. The river's water as it shooshed over the rock dam beneath the bridge smelled clean and fresh, and that surprised me, normally when I went that way for walks it wasn't so. Perhaps things were changing. A bird called once, then not again, a cuckoo, quiet, distant. I realized that if the police, if the likes of Horacio Quiñones and Jorge Aguilera Illingworth, were questioning no one but me, at least no one I knew of, then likely they were doing so because someone, someone had told them they might do well to do so. I shifted the borrowed car into first gear and, lurching at the beginning, continued on the road south around the lake, on the road toward Miguel Romero's country *villa* and whatever might await me there.

For the first couple of months at the Flying Z, my job, as Scott Geller explained it the day after Audrey and I moved up, was to spade laterals in the irrigation ditches from place to place, from time to time, to dam them below the laterals so that each section of each of the seven hay meadows flooded, received just enough of the limited water to eventually produce a nice, even crop of hay. When cut, baled, then stored, the hay would help feed the cattle, as well as the few horses (and presumably Robin's goat), throughout the winter.

Of course, I wouldn't be around for that.

Audrey, as I said earlier, "did the books." Despite my experience at Hopkins General Merchandise, I didn't know what that meant then, and despite my experience since, I don't know now. Though parts of living at the ranch seemed familiar, like Aiken and home, others, such as the nuances of its finances and Audrey's work with them, remained and will remain somehow foreign.

* * *

Asphalt, to gravel, then rutted dirt. The borrowed Mexican Ford kicked up dust, enough to embarrass me the one time I passed somebody and showered her with it, a woman with a wicker basket of mangoes balanced on her head, standing at a crossroads as if waiting to flag down a bus, as we do here. But it was late in the day for someone to be catching a bus to market, quite late. I attributed her waiting in that spot at that time, and thus being the unintentional target of the car's dust, to bad luck. Bad luck happens sometimes.

Through June and July of 1984, Audrey worked inside, I worked in the meadows. The work week went six days, Mondays we took off. Evenings, and Mondays, we took to spending with Johnny Proctor, from the sixteen-hundred acre Appaloosa ranch just south, and with Henry's daughter Robin. Johnny was tall and wide, shaggy haired and a bit bowlegged. When off for the day I'd come in from the meadows, to see Audrey, to catch some dinner, to just relax with a cold Coors draught, he'd often be waiting for me on the porch of the main house.

"Evenin', Jerry," he'd say in his hoarse but resonant baritone. "You been irrig-achin'?" And he'd put a hand to his back and say it with a wink, always with the same intonation, always as if it were just as funny the last time as it was the first. "You been workin' hard?" he'd say. "Or hardly workin'?"

I'd greet him, usually just nod to Robin, a friendly girl for a boss's daughter, a pretty girl—and that's what she was, just a girl, only eighteen when we arrived, then nineteen—pretty despite her rotund figure. She would always be sitting next to him, a hand resting perhaps too firmly, too possessively, if you were to ask me, on his forearm. At least it seemed that way. He never said, never complained.

For those first couple of months, I'd greet the two of them, put a hand to my back myself and laugh at Johnny's joke, then go inside and draw me a beer from the keg Henry always kept around.

Henry, by the way, was almost never there. In fact, I never met him, though I saw him once, just knew him through his daughter, who wasn't particularly fond of him, thought him too demanding, knew him through his wet bar and his keg of Coors and through the absurd eigh-teenth or maybe nineteenth century-type portrait of him, a hand in a coat pocket, a dog at his knee, a silver handlebar moustache dominating his face, that hung at the far end of the foyer. Whoever he was, he had a pretty nice spread.

The bar was to the left of the foyer's far end (so you had to pass Henry's portrait, at least if you wanted one of his beers to finish the day), and from it you could see through the double doors to your left again the office, my Audrey at the first desk, Susan Geller usually at the sec-ond and larger one, her husband Scott more often than not sitting next to her, done for the day himself, done at least with whatever chore might have taken him outside.

"Hay's lookin' damn good," Scott said thinly to me from his seat at that desk next to Susan one Sunday near the end of July. He tilted his hat to the rear, leaned back in his chair, folded his hands behind his neck.

I finished pouring my beer, then glanced at Audrey, who with what-ever she was doing at her desk was becoming more and more a stranger. I smiled at her, maybe looking for approval, maybe simply for a sign of recognition, then turning back to Scott said, "Thanks. I've been enjoy-ing the work." I had.

"Tomorrow," he said, "maybe the next day..."

"I can run the swather," I said, sipping foam from the top of my glass of beer, thinking of my Grandpa Herman and his problems with such equipment, but knowing, perhaps intuitively—Johnny Proctor had not yet presented to me his poet/mechanic theory of humanity—that his prob-lems would not be mine. "If it's time to cut the hay," I said confidently, "I can do it." I expected Audrey to second me in this. She didn't, rather just continued with whatever book work she was up to, whispering something now and then to Susan, effectively ignoring me. At the time, I didn't know what to attribute her silence to. It would be a few more months, some time after we had landed in Tucson, that I could even make an informed guess.

A few kilometers beyond the spot in the road where the woman had stood with her basket of mangoes I recognized to the right, toward the lake, the driveway to Miguel's *villa*, a road similar in a way, I thought as I turned into it, to the driveway of the Lubbers place back in Aiken the last time Audrey and I had visited it, knee-high weeds running down the ridge of its center.

Given that at this point I believed that my friend Miguel Romero may well be responsible for at the very least my own predicament with the police, to say nothing of the death of my friend and employee Gonzalo Méndez Paredes, I didn't really expect, say, a Brother Jarvis waiting open-handed to welcome me.

I wasn't surprised. Soon after I turned the car into what I believed to be Miguel's drive, a Guatemalan youth stood blocking my path, legs spread shoulder-width, a rifle of some sort, likely an automatic, held in both hands at the ready. I stopped the car, through the windshield he pointed his gun in my direction, scared the hell out of me, but what could I do, I'd come this far.

"I'm Jerry Hopkins," I told Miguel's young guard, leaning my head out the window, smiling toward the boy, not knowing how he'd take the smile, Christ was this the end. "I'm a friend of Miguel. *Un amigo de Miguel.*"

"*Señor* 'opkins?" the boy said, his voice hoarse, his look somehow feral, maybe it was his red eyes. Still, he tentatively lowered his rifle.

"Yes," I said, "*un vecino de* Miguel. Is he here?"

"*Espera*," he said. "He is waiting."

That disturbed me, that Miguel would know enough either of my thoughts and habits to assume I would be coming this morning, or enough of my movements, through whatever network, to know I would be.

The guard moved back, stood to the side of the narrow road, behind him a six-foot-wide prickly pear, behind that and rising slightly above him a boulder the size of a Ford F-something, opposite him and to my left a line of trees, small olive trees, transplants from somewhere in Europe. All in all, hardly a fortress. I smiled again, put the car into gear, and went.

Cutting began at the Flying Z, and I was at once surprised and not that the Hollander SpeedRower 911, Henry's only swather, operated so smoothly with me high in the driver's seat working its levers and controls.

It was rewarding work. The height of the hay showed you exactly where you started, exactly how much you'd got done. But it was exhausting work too, the days long, the heat unrelenting. Perhaps it was that aspect, coupled with Audrey and I spending less and less time with each other, continuing the trend begun in Denver, that contributed to my foolishness, the foolishness that cost me my job, and Audrey hers too, but only because she chose me over the ranch and her new friends Susan and Robin and the others.

At Henry's direction, Scott had brought in a bull for stud from the next ranch east, whose owners made a living doing that sort of thing. The bull was solid black, short-horned, stocky but smaller than I would have thought, smaller than the steers I'd seen on the ranch, or than the ranch's own bulls. Its first few days at the Flying Z, the cowboys took it to one pasture for a couple days, then the next for a couple of more, who knows how many calves they expected it to father. Or why. Especially when, again, the ranch had its own bulls who normally grazed with the rest of the herd.

The fifth day was a Monday. The cowboys, on horseback, one with a rope around the bull's horns, the other with one around its neck, brought the bull into the main complex, letting it loose in the small corral adjacent to the horse barn. I had come in fifteen or twenty minutes earlier, just finished baling the fifth of the seven meadows, and was sitting on the porch with Johnny halfway through my second beer. Robin wasn't there that day, in town picking up groceries, and Audrey, Scott, and Susan gone with her. I watched the cowboys bring the bull in, watched them turn the bull loose, watched them load their horses up then drive away. Johnny spoke:

"They're artists," he said. "Poets."

Artists I understood, but poets I didn't, and I said so.

"Jerry," he said, "there's only two kind of people."

"Give 'em to me."

"You got your poets." He took a swig of beer "And you got your mechanics."

"Poets and mechanics," I said.

"Those two are poets. They're artists."

"Beer?" I said. He handed me his glass, and I went inside and drew us two more.

We drank them, then more, washing the day's dust from our throats and our heads, talking about nothing useful, nothing in particular, we drank and talked bull through sunset and into darkness. The warm breeze from earlier shifted direction and became a cool one, the smell of horse manure faded, the refreshing aroma of hay replaced it. The others hadn't gotten back from town yet, and though we both wondered aloud where they might be, we also figured to worry was bootless. At some point we slipped into silence. Johnny was the first to break it:

"We've got to ride that animal," he said.

"What animal?"

"That goddamned bull."

"What for?"

"Cause it's waitin' for us. You ever ride one?"

Of course I hadn't, and I said so, bluntly and without embarrassment.

"Then you got to do it now. Me and you both." He downed the last of his beer, stood, and headed for the corral. I did the same, with only limited lucidity thought of possible dangers, consequences, thought of them, then quickly and dumbly dismissed them.

A three-rail whitewashed fence surrounded the corral, and a few paces ahead of me Johnny Proctor hopped it and walked calmly by the bull, who lifted its head to watch him but remained in place. Johnny opened the door to the horse barn, disappeared through it, and suddenly light from the floods above the door on each of two ten-foot posts opposite it illuminated the entire corral, turning it a surreal yellow. Johnny appeared again.

"Get on in here," he said, and after a second or two pause I climbed over the fence myself, deliberately and quickly, trying to make up, I suppose, for my initial hesitation. Once upright on the corral's dirt floor, I stayed next to the fence. The bull, fifteen feet from me, ten from Johnny, looked from him to me then back, snorted, walked its hind legs around until it faced us both, more or less. "Walk toward it," Johnny said, "and heads up, it's gonna want to put up a fight." I moved, though slowly. "If he comes your way, step to the side and go for his horns, both hands."

I took a couple of more steps, then suddenly felt lights on the right side of my face, turned toward them and saw they were headlights, one set, no, two. I thought *caught, busted*, then stunned turned back to see Johnny Proctor wrestling that stud bull, oblivious to the headlights and what they meant, his arms wrapped around its head, his hands clutching its horns, the heels of his boots dug in and kicking up dust as the bull fought, ran. Moments later Scott was hollering over the fence for me to get the hell out of there, then when Johnny had let go and slapped me on the back and I had followed him out over the top rail, it was suddenly Scott and me standing in the headlights and the dust the two trucks had churned up, Scott calling me on the carpet, yelling, "Fuckin' with the boss's property, no wonder the damn thing ain't been producing, you been doing this every night out on the range?" And then Boss Henry, the only time I'd ever see him, leaning forward onto the hood of his pick-up, staring at us, looking different without the moustache, but still him. "Shit," Scott was saying, then, "Don't be surprised if I let you go in the morning," which he did, of course, had to, with Henry seeing and all. Had to, he said, you couldn't have the help fucking with the property, "specially in plain sight of the boss."

The night pretty much ended there, at least as far as Johnny, Scott, Henry, the others and the bull (I assume) were concerned. Back in our trailer, Audrey and I made love that night, a couple of times. Best I can figure, that very well may have been the evening little Moses was conceived. Her passion puzzled me. It seemed to have been brought on by my having stood in the corral with that bull, by my courage and my bravery, certainly not by my foolishness, my stupidity. Who can explain women?

Whatever, by that time the next night we'd loaded the F-100 and headed west, been asleep for an hour in a rest area near Rawlins, decided that this time our ultimate destination would be Arizona, first a visit to her parents somewhere in Phoenix, then who knew where, maybe further south. It was time, we decided as we drove out the ranch's dirt road towards the highway, to maybe use some of my dead father's money to set ourselves up somewhere, to make somewhere home.

Miguel's *villa* as I approached it had what appeared to be guards at its front door, slim young men dressed in green camouflage and heavily armed. They were standing at attention, and I wondered if that was for my benefit—likely they had known I was coming as well, certainly had seen the Ford's dust announcing me—or if they held themselves that way all the time, good little soldiers, so full of themselves. Who knew if one of them, or the boy out by the road, had been the one to put the bullet through Gonzalo's head? The thought chilled me, as you might imagine, giving me goosebumps and a shudder.

The road ended in a circular drive fronting the house and the guards and surrounding a rock-and-cactus garden about thirty feet in diameter. I pulled into the drive to the right, went about halfway around, and parked. When I shut the engine off, it dieseled, sputtered, then stopped, a stark contrast to the silence that followed. Although, as I remembered, Miguel's *villa* didn't sit directly on Lake Atitlán, the path which led to the lake from the back porch was no more than a quarter of a mile long. I could smell the lake. Strong, fishy, but still clean, as the river had surprisingly struck me earlier.

The sun shone bright, coming over my right shoulder. It turned the white of the house into a blinding white, a white capped by semi-circular terra cotta shingles, but that sun was at a high enough angle that the porch between and behind the guards, the house's entrance, stayed in deep black shadow. I heard Miguel open the door and step out onto the porch before I saw him, then, and I'm not embarrassed to say that not being able to see if or what he might be carrying, I was trembling, I could feel it all down through, thought I might piss my pants, though I didn't.

"Good morning, Jerry," I heard Miguel say, still invisible, voice calm. "It's a good morning for a drive in the country, wouldn't you say?"

"Morning, Miguel." I stared into the darkness, uneasy that he could see me but I not him, still I stared, hoping my eyes would adjust and things would somehow even up and if he was going to shoot me I'd be able to see him do it. "You seem pretty well-protected," I said. No shots came. I realized that except to speak I hadn't taken a breath since I'd gotten out of the car, so I took one, a deep one, took a long, deep, filling breath.

"You know how it fuckin' is." He stepped out into the sunlight, no more than ten or twelve feet from me. His black-rimmed glasses seemed to occupy half his face. He looked unarmed, his right hand stuffed to the knuckles into the pocket of his jeans, his left curled around a tall, frosted glass, three-fourths full. A tiny orange and yellow umbrella leaned up incongruously out of it. He was smiling, not quite a sneer, but close to it.

"We need to talk, Miguel," I said.

"About what, mi amigo?" he said, as if he didn't know, he who had been waiting for me, expecting me. He was going to make me say it, to name it, him, not going to make anything easy.

"Gonzalo," I said. "Of course."

"It's too bad about Gonzalo, too fuckin' bad, isn't it? You find somebody to take his place?"

I didn't answer, figured he knew. "He was my friend, you know."

"If you say so, though from what I hear, for a friend you didn't seem to know too goddamn much about him." He took a swallow from his glass, and suddenly it was only one-fourth full. "Look, Jerry." Still smiling. "We all lose friends. Other 'ords, and I don't mean to be mean about it, that's fuckin' life."

I had been sweating and was beginning to feel it, under my arms, on my chest, my forehead.

It wasn't that hot.

I pulled my wet shirt away from my chest, with my hand wiped from my forehead back across the slick bald crown to my neck. I noticed that the kid standing to my right, Miguel's left, was really bug-eyed, black irises surrounded by bright white circles, and I vaguely recalled from somewhere that that might be a condition that had a name, one which of course I couldn't remember and wasn't important now anyway. I'd better pay attention. This might be serious.

"That's life, Jerry, fuckin' life," Miguel was saying, and he might have said something before that I'd missed. "Best to just accept it, take what comes your way."

"I'd like to do that, Miguel. But the police. Not just Horacio, but Aguilera Illingworth too. They're asking me questions. They're acting like I'm suspect number one."

"They have jobs to do."

"They're friends of yours, aren't they? Horacio, that fucking Colonel."

"So what is it, Jerry? You want me to put in a word for you? Tell them you didn't do it, you couldn't have, not somebody like you?"

I'm not sure where it came from, if it came from so many years of being pushed and pushed by people and events and even history, progress, being so passive that I rarely pushed back. That I'd left Aiken and everywhere in between Aiken and Tela rather than stop, stand and say, No, this is home, I'm not going. That person after person—my sisters and their families, Stevie Lubbers and his, Audrey, little Moses, even the one-footed Vietnam vet Norman Wright, for Christ's sake, even Norma with her rat dog Red—that person after person in my life had become or was becoming nothing more than a subject for my writing, whether that writing was to be for the Hopkins family journals or something else uncertain. Would Gonzalo just be another in a long line? Would Carmela be next, or Nati? Maybe the time might have come for me to stand up and say, No, this person's important, this person means something to me.

Maybe. Maybe I had simply been so shamed by Nati's courage compared to my own apparent cowardice that I had to do *something.*

Maybe, all in all, I was just never a very bright guy and my stupidity was finally catching up with me.

Whatever, when Miguel said, "So what is it, Jerry? You want me to put in a word for you? Tell them you didn't do it, you couldn't have, not somebody like you?" I answered this way:

"What it is, motherfucker, is that we need to talk, just you and me, face to face, away from your goons here, and I think you're being pretty goddamn rude thinking we're going to stand out here and you're going to insult me and I'm going to take it and that's going to be that."

Miguel lost his smile—it hadn't been much of one anyway—said something in quick Spanish to his boys, made hand motions as if shooing them away. They went, with puzzled looks, ran rifle-toting out into the sparse woods, who knew where. He tossed the rest of his drink into the sand at his feet, and with the other hand removed his glasses.

"Inside, then," Miguel said. "Won't you join me?" He opened the front door and entered, I followed, scared. Fucking scared.

CHAPTER XVII
REMEMBER THE MAINE

February 20th, 1898

It is Sunday, a warm, sunny Sunday of a cold, cold winter, and my grandsons Carter and Thomas Nelson have gone for wood. They have taken Carter's wife Mary, pregnant with child, and Carter's three children with them, making a day of it. Such outings are good if not made too much a habit.

My son Francis and his stoic wife Jane have gone to Mount Vernon for the day. I am here alone. The store is of course closed. On the table before me lies an edition of the New York Journal, *Thursday, February 17th. It is one of Hearst's papers. A glance at its inflammatory headlines would make that apparent to anyone literate these sad days:*

"DESTRUCTION OF THE WARSHIP MAINE WAS THE WORK OF AN ENEMY,"

"Assistant Secretary Roosevelt Convinced the Explosion of the War Ship Was Not an Accident,"

"The Journal offers $50,000 Reward for the Conviction of the Criminals Who Sent 258 American Sailors to Their Death,"

"$50,000 REWARD! for the Detection of the Perpetrator of the Maine Outrage!"

Hearst and his capitalist cronies have markets to keep open, trade to protect. To do so they want our country to wage war, they want nothing less, and to get their war and achieve their sinister objectives they are making the Cuban question a question of honor, of bravery.

These are not powerless men ignorant of what they do. They will most certainly get their way, will most certainly be responsible for the premature deaths of hundreds, if not thousands, of Americans, Cubans, Spaniards, and others. Their own sons will not die, of course, but our sons will, knowing only in their last moments, if at all, that they and their parents and their countrymen who so flippantly sent them to their deaths have once again confused bravery with stupidity. These sons may find, too, that they themselves are not free from culpability.

Sometimes it becomes clearer and clearer that the human race, top to bottom, is not a particularly bright one. God have mercy on it. God have mercy on us, on all of us, on all our stupid, mortal souls. Perhaps one day soon death will free me from humanity's hopeless folly.

Benjamin Harrison Hopkins

My ancestor Benjamin Harrison Hopkins got one of his wishes, the wish most explicit. With his son Francis he died a couple of months after he made that entry, he died in a horse-and-buggy runaway on what would decades later become Highway 13. It was he, through his words in this perceptive though bitter journal entry, who finally was foremost in my thoughts as last Thursday I followed Miguel Roberts inside through the front door of his *villa* in the countryside south of Tela.

We entered to a blue-and-white-tiled foyer, paneled walls and a low ceiling, an oak combination hall tree and umbrella stand half blocking our way. Miguel in front of me walked quickly toward the back and some other room, a room brighter than where we were. In his left hand he held his glasses, in his right the empty highball glass. That he so obviously felt he could turn his back on me without worry pissed me off, at first offended me, then I remembered that here in Tela I held a reputation as a nice, easy going guy. I had cultivated that and was even proud of it. I couldn't very well suddenly expect someone to see me, to think of me, differently, as someone to be wary of.

We reached one room, the bright one with its great windows opening up on the lake side of house, passed through it and into a close, dark, windowless room to its left. A yellow beanbag chair, of all things, and a turquoise and bone-white dinette set, fifties style in its right angles, two chairs where there once might have been four, were the room's only furniture. Miguel sat in the dinette chair nearest the far wall, a stucco wall whose paint, I couldn't help but notice, was peeling in more places than I could, if I'd had such an inclination, count.

Setting his glasses upside down on the table in front of him, "Sit," he said. "Here or there, I don't give a rat's fuckin' ass."

"I'd rather stand."

"You'd rather." He slung his empty glass casually but forcefully against the wall to my left, his right, and it struck dead center a whitish rectangle where a painting must have until recently hung. The glass shattered, loudly, piercingly, the shards falling clinking to the floor, a floor covered by a wrinkled, brown indoor-outdoor carpet, stained in places, large stains whose colors I couldn't quite make out. The glass shattered, and one or two shards lightly and harmlessly struck my legs.

"Was that supposed to scare me?" I said, and I started to fold my arms across my chest, but that seemed somehow as if it might hamper my readiness for what might come. I let my arms hang at my sides and flexed my fingers. I don't know why, and though I expected Miguel to laugh at me for it, to mock me, he didn't. "Maybe I should be scared, Miguel. You killed Gonzalo, God knows why, you or one of your shits out there. You killed him and for some reason you've got something in for me."

"You don't think I'm going to sit here and make some confession, do you?" He laughed as he spoke. "Mr. fuckin' Perry Mason."

"You don't need to. I don't care. I imagine somehow he got in the way of you and your CIA buddies and your little army games. Had the wrong idea of how to go about life."

Miguel said nothing, and I took his silence as an admission of guilt. Damn him.

I'd been standing near center of the room, and I moved back slightly, moved back towards, more or less, the door through which we'd entered. I stopped when I felt my heel meet the wall. A quick glance showed the door a yard to my right. "I don't know if you and the Colonel are in it together," I said, "or if you just put him onto me because you all need someone to blame and I'm easy. I don't know, and I don't care."

Miguel leaned forward, placed his stubby hands on his stout knees. "You can just forget about it, Jerry, you know you can just fuckin' forget about it and it'll all be over soon. They'll know you didn't do shit, you couldn't have, not somebody like you. They'll write it off as just another fuckin' terrorist killed by one of his own. They do it all the time."

"What did he do that was so goddamn awful?"

"He was a fuckin' rebel, like I said, ain't that enough? Christ, Jerry, just forget about it. Gonzalo was a rebel, and now he's out of the way. Quit and it'll all be over soon. They'll know you didn't do shit, you couldn't have, not somebody like you. Quiñones and Aguilera need someone to investigate for the killings, they got motions they got to go through. Let 'em do it. Just go back and run your restaurant and let 'em do it. It'll blow over, they'll know you couldn't have killed Gonzalo and they'll just file his death unsolved."

"Gonzalo was my friend."

"We went through this out front." He sighed and straightened his thick body, appearing to roll his eyes, perhaps, though, only appearing to.

"I didn't have to know his whole life history to like him," I said.

"I don't need this, Jerry. I got enough worry without you making shit."

I wanted to say something then, something like, *You've got more worry coming, buddy, you can't just kill somebody and get away with it, you can't just kill my friend and expect me to lie back and silently watch. We Hopkins men, we generations of Hopkins men, we aren't like that,* I wanted to say, though I wasn't at all sure it would be true, felt more certain than not that it wouldn't be.

So I said nothing.

Just like me, Audrey would tell you.

"Go on home," said Miguel, and he was again leaning forward as if ready to stand, spring, maybe attack. "Don't make me," he said, but as he said it he seemed once more to lean back a little, to relax. Was this a decoy, was he trying to lull me to sleep?

"I can't," I said, hearing the finality of the words even as I spoke them, feeling that finality, me and Stevie Lubbers had lobbed our grenades over the canal, we'd attacked the German soldiers, we'd begun the assault on the enemy and now we had to follow it up, we had to cross the canal and finish what we'd begun and we did, but no, Stevie was in Boston, I was alone across Aiken's canal, and even as the sudden whoosh of the water behind me, the radiation-hot water filling the canal and likely making it some Rubicon, even as that water scared me, scared the hell out of me, I realized I hadn't really fathomed what our young boys' attack might mean, what consequences such an action might produce and demand.

And I think my realization was a good thing.

"I can't," I had to tell Miguel and did, no Stevie around, no Hopkins men, my father and my grandfathers and all those haunting ones before, no Audrey or Randy Proctor or anybody, just me alone. "I can't let you get away with it."

Miguel pushed to his feet and lunged toward me, his hands and arms extended in front of him. I can't say it was a surprise. I moved left, not particularly deftly, but enough so. He missed, turned, came at me again, more quickly than I would have thought his chunkiness capable of. I dodged again, he again missed, but now I was back in the corner, the beanbag chair to my right, the table and chairs to my left, Miguel between me and the door, panting, loudly panting. The morning drink?

He was in a high crouch, poised like a wrestler, arms at his sides. His left hand was open, but the fingers of his right curled around the handle of a knife, a seven or eight-inch blade on it, all told over a foot long. I hadn't seen him pull it, and I suddenly realized this was a fight I couldn't win, he was too quick, he was a killer, he knew how to do it, and I was just me.

"Hold on, Miguel," I said, and I heard my voice shake, knowing that couldn't be good. "Let's talk."

"We could talk now, I could talk to you now, motherfucker." As Miguel spoke, his voice sure and steady, he blinked, hard. "But I couldn't trust you not to talk again later, could I?" He blinked again, again hard, as if he had something irritable, painful in his eyes, eyes I hadn't realized before were so tiny, so beady, so appropriately, villainously beady. "You've got to go, Jerry. I wish you hadn't made me."

It hit me then that Miguel wasn't looking at me, at least not directly, but those beady, blinking eyes were looking rather at my ear or something, at something over my shoulder. I wanted to turn and look myself, but I knew there was nothing there, I had seen that empty wall just seconds before, and it hit me, hit me like a sack of hammers that without his glasses Miguel couldn't really see me, couldn't see anything, could only look where he thought I was.

With my right foot I kicked at the beanbag chair, then fell back to my left in time to miss the blade-first lunge. I landed against the wall, still standing. He tripped over the chair, the knife flying from his hand to fall quietly at my feet, and he landed face first on the hard carpeted floor. He grunted, and didn't move, I didn't think it at the time but figure now he must have had the wind knocked out of him.

I dropped onto his back, digging my knees into his shoulders blades. He gasped near silently, struggled only minimally, slight writhes puzzling, again, in their slightness. But I couldn't stop to consider pity—Christ, he intended to kill me—and I wrapped my fingers around his thick neck, wrapped them tightly, I felt for the Adam's apple and when my fingertips reached the knob of it, I squeezed.

It took forever. His gasps began to alternate irregularly with gags, sickening, wet, gurgling gags. For a brief few moments I felt his legs kick, his body lurch in struggle, but that ended, and sometime later all smaller signs of life left as well.

And as I continued to kneel on him, continued to squeeze, I knew Miguel was dead, *muerto. Y lo hube matado*, I had killed him. It didn't feel good. What should have been a relief wasn't. I took no pride in something like bravery—clearly that hadn't played a part in it—but neither did I feel shame for my stupidity, though that may have. I wanted to cry, but didn't.

I let go of his neck and stood, and with my foot shoved him over onto his back to make sure he was dead. His black eyes were stuck open, and it would be easy to say that they stared at me, stared hauntingly and accusingly, but they didn't. They were dead, and they weren't staring at anything. I've heard the word blue used to describe how he looked—BLUE IN THE FACE comes to mind, though I don't recall the context—but it wasn't quite a blue, rather more a soft purple, not a bad color in another circumstance, a nice color, say, for a young black-haired, brown-skinned Mayan woman's summer morning dress.

I retraced my steps from earlier through the house to the front door, then out across the rock garden to the car. Miguel's two men, wherever they had run to, apparently hadn't come back. I saw sign of no one. The sun hadn't moved, shadows were all in the same places, at the same angles, as though time hadn't passed. The only change was that the air smelled different, not clean, not foul, not anything. Perhaps the wind had shifted.

I started the borrowed car, it started easily but still ran roughly, and I drove out. The young guard still stood at his post by the road, and I waved as I passed. He waved back. Or maybe he saluted.

Out on the road and headed toward Tela I thought, of all people, of old Miss What's-her-name, the teacher back in Aiken, about when she'd had a heart attack the night before she was to take us on a field trip to the Indian mounds in Newark. The trip had been canceled, she had been taken to a hospital there instead, where she died. I remembered lamenting that dead or not, she had at least gotten to go somewhere.

Well now, I thought, so had I.

And look what it had come to.

I crossed the *Río Tela*—like *el lago* it too was odorless, maybe it wasn't the wind, maybe just me—and returned the borrowed car to my jeweler acquaintance. I thanked him, said I owed him one, and walked through the bare streets the direction of the lake, toward Daddy Rabbit's. I hoped my borrowing his car and then killing a man while it was in my possession wouldn't cause him any trouble.

Inside a quiet Daddy Rabbit's, I greeted Nati, asked about Edelberto and heard he was still doing fine, which came as no surprise, it hadn't been much more than an hour since I'd last asked. I took a beer from the cooler, a dark Moza, and went to my usual chair in the corner, my usual table. I sat and waited. For the lunch rush in case I was needed. For a visit from Quiñones, or maybe from Aguilera Illingworth, maybe both, a last visit, this time not on so polite a level. For the spray of bullets as Miguel's boys took their revenge.

I sat, drank my beer, and waited.
Sometimes a man has to stop running.

CHAPTER XVIII
HOLY HOPE

Here, finally, may be what it's about:

Miguel wasn't the first person I'd killed.

A few weeks after leaving Wyoming, Audrey and I entered Phoenix on an Interstate highway, early September, early afternoon. On the freeway Tempe, then Chandler. We passed through Chandler, then on to Apache Junction, the town which Noah and Naomi Marsh had retired to.

The month on the road had been characterized by silence, anger, and resentment on Audrey's part. It was all understandable, and I accepted it best I could. I had ruined much.

Directions, which Audrey, finally smiling for a second as the wind blew her gray hair back, received over a phone outside a Circle K, took us north into the foothills of the Superstition Mountains, finally to Distant Horizons, the Marshes' trailer park. The park appeared to be professionally landscaped, several kinds of cactus, several colors of gravel. No grass lawns, of course, a few trees, but those mostly decorative oranges and lemons, none over ten feet or so high. Easy-to-read green and white street signs made the trailer simple to find. When we reached it, and after Audrey had double-checked and told me stiffly, Yes, this is it, we parked the old pick-up on the street. We had barely gotten out and on our feet, no time to stretch, when Noah's bass voice boomed from somewhere behind the trailer:

"We're in the back," he yelled. "By the pool."

A pool, indeed any water, sounded good. The desert in August can be very hot for the uninitiated. Within half an hour we had joined them,

them with their brown, wrinkled skin and their frozen strawberry margaritas and their wide, white-toothed grins.

How things change.

We had hugged them and told them how good they looked and how much we'd missed them. We had complimented their trailer, with its screened porch out front and its redwood deck in the back, its waist-high, spear-leaved agave, its well-placed clumps of tall pampas grass, grass the color of brown mustard. We had done that, then me in shorts, Audrey in shorts and a t-shirt, we'd taken the drinks they'd offered and, within half an hour of our arrival, we were standing neck-deep in their pool, leaning against its side, singing as if nothing had happened. The four of us singing, singing in four-part the song that Audrey and I so long ago had sung as a duet:

"To-day He lives, bring-ing us Sal-va-tion..."

Noah took bass, me baritone, and since both Audrey and her mother were natural altos, a short argument had preceded those first lines coming forth, but Audrey being the younger had quickly yielded and was now giving the higher soprano part her best strained shot.

"To-day he lives, all hope to give..."

They asked how long we'd be staying. Though, I'm sure, I was expected to answer for both of us, I took an icy sip of my drink and kept silent, deferring to Audrey, who said not long, we thought we might move on to Tucson, set up shop of some sort there, we'd heard good things.

In fact, we'd heard nothing of Tucson, from no one, anywhere. A half hour and Audrey'd had enough. You had to like her for it, the last few weeks notwithstanding.

"To-day I know," we sang, "He holds the fu-ture..."

Chlorine from the pool's water made for strange-tasting strawberries. Beneath its surface I placed my hand low on Audrey's back. She stiffened, moved slightly away.

"And life will be worth liv-ing," we sang, "be-cause to-day He lives."

Christ.

We stayed with the Marshes the better part of three weeks. We then drove the hundred-plus hot miles down to Tucson, where we stayed our first few nights at the Ghost Ranch Lodge, a one-story Best Western on

Miracle Mile, another couple of hundred or so of my dead father's dollars gone for it. We figured that while we stayed there we would look for work, for a place to live.

In those days, those few days, Audrey wouldn't let me touch her. During our time with her parents, she had been growing even more irritable, short for no apparent reason, talking little to her parents, not at all to me. Of course I assumed her attitude toward her parents grew out of her attitude toward me, and that the distance she was keeping between us and thus between her and them was due to her having grown tired of me, of putting up with me and my restlessness with a lack of direction, of my stupidity in losing the job in Wyoming, in who knew what before that. Was she blaming me now for everything before? The drop in business at Hopkins General Merchandise, the subsequent move from Aiken? The meaningless jobs that followed—in Granville, Columbus, then in Denver and on the Wyoming ranch?

She may have been wondering, I must have thought as we lay in the clean-smelling queen-sized bed of the Ghost Ranch Lodge's room one-one-something, a wall between us thick like oil, maybe 20W-50, silent and invisible like a window pane or like guilt itself creeping up and suddenly becoming smothering, she may have been wondering what the hell was coming next, what meaningless action masquerading as meaningful work, as life, would descend on her next and sling her hopelessly one way or another.

It was our third night there. I had hit on what seemed an excellent employment prospect at a local liquor store chain, a company always seeking energetic assistant managers, the ad had said and the kid who interviewed me had echoed. The pay sounded weak, but adequate for the time being, enough to get us by (with occasional aid from savings) until promotions came, until whatever boss I ended up working for might say, *This man, Mr. Hopkins, he's no youngster but he knows the business, we can use him, he can make us money. Put him in charge.*

Lying in that bed, I finally broke the silence and told Audrey again what work might be coming.

"Fuck you," she said, and all anxieties I'd felt and I've voiced now though not so much then seemed confirmed.

"It's nothing, isn't it?" I said. "Just one more dead end. This new job's nothing."

"You don't understand, Jerry. You don't know anything."

"I love you," I said, something I'd pulled out from time to time over our years together, something that, as we all know, means less, much less, said than acted. Of course a poet would know this, would know that showing was almost always more effective than telling, but I wasn't one, wasn't a poet, never had been.

"I'm pregnant, you shit," she said, and opposite me in the bed she sounded so far away, so very far away.

"Are you sure?" I said, stunned, of course.

"You can be such a moron. Haven't you noticed anything? Do I have to spell it all out for you?"

"Well, I thought you seemed—"

"Yeah, you thought. And yes, I'm sure, my period's late, very late, very fucking late."

I'd never known her to swear so much. I said, "A baby."

"Yeah, a fucking baby, and us with no insurance."

"We have some money left," I said, "some of my father's money. Most of it, in fact."

"Christ, Jerry. You don't understand anything. It's not the money, it's not the insurance."

I thought for a minute. When our conversation had begun, she had been facing away from me, toward the TV built into its box of gray, rough-cut wood, toward the print of a large-eyed, sad-eyed Indian girl in traditional dress on the wall behind it. She had since turned toward me, but the gulf between us had not narrowed.

I said, "If it's not the insurance, Audrey, then what the hell is it?"

She looked into my eyes, her own eyes gray and small, her long, brittle hair gray, her nightgown, her skin gray, gray and somehow foreign, and said, "It's you, goddamn it, it's you. It's us. We can't have a baby. We've got no home. We've got no business, got no business doing it."

That made sense—instinctively, perhaps, you think roots, the Hopkins name, the place, the tradition of the journals matter—and at the same time it made no sense at all, having a home hadn't seemed to do us much good, me or her, hadn't seemed to make much difference about who we were. Having a place to call home hadn't made us better people, and being homeless, so to speak, the last couple of years hadn't made us worse. I said as much.

"Christ, Jerry," she said, and her voice was shaking, with tears or anger, I couldn't tell which and turned away, toward another portrait on another wall. I couldn't make myself look at her. "I don't like you," she said, "I don't like you anymore. And I sure as hell don't want to be the mother of your baby. At least not now."

I was shaken, of course, though I had seen much of this coming. Not the baby, but the other, the dislike, the loathing, the end it all represented. I slid out of the bed and into a pair of jeans I had left lying on the floor. I went to the bathroom and looked at myself in the mirror, balding at thirty-two, beard scraggly like that of a vagrant. I'm not sure I liked what I saw. Certainly my father at the same age had been something more. Whatever, I didn't dwell on it, just splashed some tepid tap water on my face and dug my fingers into the corners of my eyes to clean them out, returned to the main room where the stranger Audrey pregnant with my son or daughter lay distant. I pulled on a t-shirt, slipped on my tennis shoes, and went alone out the door into the cool and dry desert night, out onto Miracle Mile, where the only traffic all seemed headed in the same direction, towards a bowling alley west of the motel, white headlights to red tail lights, white headlights to red tail lights.

Across the street there seemed to be no lights at all, white, orange neon, or otherwise, no businesses of any sort. The nothingness appealed to me, perhaps a matter of like drawn to like, so at a gap in the sparse traffic I crossed. I walked east, quickly at first. As my eyes adjusted to the darkness, I realized I was walking next to a cemetery, on the other side of that wrought-iron fence to my left.

It wasn't a cemetery like that adjacent to the church in Aiken, with its headstones laid out in concentric half-circles, mimicking each other in size and height, in distance apart. The monuments here, even in the darkness, were different whites and grays and blacks of granite and marble, some tall and pointed like obelisks, some short and squat and modest, markers only, some clearly casket-sized above-ground tombs. For the first time since my days at Davidson Hardware with its Uncle Fred's Quick Liquid Rat Poison, I wished that somewhere, somewhere if not here, some stone were standing with me beneath it, marking my own grave, a stone with nothing more than my name, Gerard Manley Hopkins (not the fucking poet), my date of birth, 1952, and the date of my death, 1984, carved neatly or not into it.

I reached the cemetery's entrance, read its name in black wrought iron above the padlocked gate as Holy Hope, and had to wonder bitterly what the hell that might mean. Christ, the folks were dead, the time for hope had passed. I sat on the cold sidewalk, sat cross-legged, buried my head in my hands, and cried. Not hard, just soft sobs, not long, just a couple of sobs, just briefly, that was that.

"I didn't mean to hurt you," I heard Audrey say from somewhere above me, her voice now soft and caring but still carrying an unforgiving edge. I looked up. She was there, her face in shadow but her hair flaring in the street lights haloing it and now white and ghost-like. She had followed me. "It's just the truth," she said. "I don't mean to hurt you, but Christ."

"I know," I said, and I thought I did, and I thought for a second I would talk to Audrey, we'd talk, as adults we'd come to some sensible agreement about what to do with us, with the two of us, with this baby.

But then a car pulled to the curb behind her, a rumbling Detroit car chrome-shining with the stereo inside it rumbling louder, and a thick bare arm reached out of a suddenly open door to grab her, grab her nightgown, and a man's drunken voice was yelling, commanding, "Get in the car, bitch," and without fear, with only anger, I was up quicker than I could have imagined and breaking that arm like a dry branch across my knee, and like I was some strong guy I was pulling the man or boy who had yelled obscenely at my wife out onto the concrete by his now-broken arm, then I was kicking him as he lay, lay screaming, then crying, writhing, curling up to cover himself uselessly.

I was merciless, I wouldn't stop kicking him with my tennis shoes now bloody, my toes within them now likely broken, but Christ he deserved it, how dare he, and not long after I thought that thought, the car squealed off with the driver yelling something in a Spanish accent, an accent notable not for how the man pronounced his words, but more for how even in his disbelieving hysteria he was careful to pronounce them correctly, yelling something like, "The motherfucker's crazy, fucking crazy." And soon after, me still kicking, the man cowering on the sidewalk beneath me stopped moving, and I suddenly realized Audrey beside me wasn't screaming as I thought she had been, maybe that was just something inside my head, and I kicked again, then again, then again, and I saw the man's eyes were open, stuck open seemed to be, though the black, red and white eyeball of one looked to be hanging out onto his cheek, and that seemed odd, but I spread my arms to my sides for balance and I kicked again. It seemed then I had to.

"You can stop now, Jerry," I heard Audrey whisper, though I couldn't say then and can't say now that I recognized her voice, or even that she did indeed whisper. "You can stop now," she said, perhaps somewhat urgently, and slowly, after one last soft kick, I did, I did stop, and I saw that the man on the sidewalk couldn't be alive after that, I knelt down to him and pain sliced through my knees, especially the right one, the knee of the leg I had used most, and the man's breath, though he wasn't breathing now, stunk like liquor and something else, maybe like the rot my father had reeked of in his last years.

No, as long as I'd known him.

This man, this rude and maybe dangerous stranger, looking at him I thought he may have only been a boy, was dead, clearly dead. No life to him. In my family I had seen death before, so I knew.

As I knelt above him, I looked around, across the street to the strip of mostly dark motels, no people, no eyes that I could see, looked east and west on Miracle Mile, no traffic, none, who knew why, behind us into the Holy Hope cemetery, of course nothing there, no life, no hope. I turned my eyes up to Audrey, and though still I didn't recognize her, nor, I assume, she me, enough passed between us that we silently returned to our room, across the silent street, the cool night air now turned cold as sweat evaporated.

The next day we moved ourselves east, into the guest house of a desert *villa* in the foothills of the Santa Catalinas, and we never spoke of the incident again.

Killing someone changes you into another person. New uncertainties replace old ones. Fresh fears appear from nowhere to clutch at you, to beg for attention. You feel like you lose some of your identity, which is quite a thing to lose when you've spent so much time fumbling with it anyway. You want to whisper *I am Jerry, Gerard Manley Hopkins*, and you want to scream it, too. *I am Jerry Hopkins, and you can't do anything to me, not now*, and you want to believe it. But you end up more lost than ever, more vulnerable.

It's no fun.

Audrey and I had our opportunities to speak of the incident, though not that many. I had killed the man in early September, and by January, pregnant Audrey and I had split up. Till then, I worked for that chain of liquor stores, Audrey stayed home at the rented guest house and sewed. After we split, I kept my job, and she kept up her sewing and as in Columbus a couple of years earlier made a few dollars doing it. I roomed with some kids near the university, helped her with the apartment, she stayed at the guest house. The county took care of her pre-natal.

In April the boy was born. She called me from the hospital, said he was a boy, was healthy. Said she would name him Moses, after the Biblical brother of the namesake of her ancestor Aaron Marsh, the man whose existence the Hopkins family journals had revealed to her and to her family. I felt good for him, for my son. His name wouldn't be a typical Hopkins name, neither would it be that of a poet. He wouldn't have to live with that curse.

Of course like those of his maternal ancestors, though, his would be a Biblical name, and perhaps thus carry some baggage I wasn't aware of. I could only hope that baggage would be a cross he could bear, so to speak, Biblically.

Audrey said she would go on AFDC, at least for the time being.

"Not long," she said, the last time I spoke with her. "I'll find good work. I've met someone here, a friend of the landlord. He needs a book-keeper." She had gotten by okay so far, I guess, doing whatever she was doing, at least she'd never complained. As always, I trusted her to know what way was best.

I asked her if I should come see the baby at the hospital, and she said, Sure, if I'd like to. I said I didn't know, and then at the liquor store I met the Guatemalan man who owned Daddy Rabbit's before me, owned it when it was still called MARIO'S and had been closed for nearly a year. He lived in Tucson now, would be buying his vodka at our store, and he sold me the restaurant cheap, took a bit over half of what was left of my dead father's money, but still cheap, told me the bus that would get me there, told me who in Tela to see to get set up.

I bought and paid, wrangled (there's that western talk again) a promise from a fellow I worked with that he'd deliver the Le Sabre I'd traded my father's old truck for to Audrey, and within a week I'd left Arizona and the states without ever seeing Moses, without seeing Audrey again.

I can't imagine doing that. In retrospect I can't believe I would do it again under the same circumstances. Also I can't imagine Audrey letting me go so easily. But likely her silent complicity produced a guilt of its own, one that froze her into inaction and maybe still does. It may be why she didn't pressure me those years ago to stay, why she hasn't since to return, to become our son's father.

She knows.

Killing someone can change your life, make you do things you never thought you'd do. Things you couldn't imagine.

CHAPTER XIX
IT'TH GOD, AGAIN

Today is mail day in Tela. Not that we only get mail one day a week, or one day a month, or whatever the term "mail day" might seem to imply. It's just that most mail, and not just that from overseas or up in the states, gets caught in a traffic jam, so to speak, somewhere in our country's postal bureaucracy. And though someone, in our case Jaime Quiñones, a younger brother of our police chief Horacio Quiñones, delivers mail almost daily, he only really has much of anything to deliver on Wednesdays, a day or so after someone else in some substation in Guatemala City has discovered the jam and released, like puzzling yellow pus from a painless infection, all the mail somehow held up there for the previous several days.

No. To say all the mail would be to exaggerate. If it all came through, what would our someone at the substation over in Guatemala City have to do till he got *his* next shipment, held up wherever it may be?

No, not all. Just enough let through to keep the customers satisfied, just enough held back to give our man something to continue to sort, to look at, to wonder about then inexplicably forget.

However our system here works, today, Wednesday, mail day, I got many letters. Early this afternoon, Nati and Carmela and Edelberto were running Daddy Rabbit's, and I was at my house prone on my couch in the front room trying to get some rest. I'd killed Miguel Friday, five days ago, and no one had come for me, no one had come to question, to arrest, to exact revenge. Of course I worried. But of course me being who I am I couldn't make myself seek out any of my potential adversaries, confront them before they me. And with that worry still nagging at me, then, sleep the last five nights had been hard to come by.

"Señor 'opkins," a voice came through my open front window. It was Jaime's but I didn't recognize it at first, him only coming around once a week, and that usually to the restaurant, where his voice might blend in with many others and thus lose its distinctiveness. I lifted my head, blacksmith anvil-heavy, off my arms and looked. I saw his square face, a face dominated by a genuinely cheerful smile, in the corner of the window. Just the face at first, a face unconnected. No torso, no neck, no arms. I thought I must be dreaming and let my head fall back down. "Señor 'opkins!" he said again "El correo. Cartas! Tengo cartas, para usted!"

I lifted my head, looked again, now I could see an arm as well as a head, and that made more sense, though not much more. He was holding some letters up, waving them, excitement accelerating toward urgency. "Is it today?" I said.

"Sí, Señor 'opkins. El correo!"

I made myself get up, managed to smile at him as my fatigued body walked itself to the window. He handed me the letters, and I took them. "Thanks," I said. "Gracias." The man lived for these days, for times like this. No point in letting him down. I remembered Aiken, I knew what it was like to get excited about nothing, having little choice through times in your life but to do so.

"Ha visto su vecino?" he said, and I saw he was holding another bundle of letters in his left hand, and the hand kept eerily twitching as if on its own it knew it had to deposit its letters somewhere, somewhere. "Ha visto su vecino?" he said, and I saw he was holding another bundle of letters in his left hand, and the hand kept eerily twitching as if on its own it knew it had to deposit its letters somewhere, somewhere. "Ha visto Señor Romero?"

I felt myself shudder. Had his brother Horacio put him up to that question, to asking me if I'd seen Miguel? Maybe, maybe not. Either way, I was into the fifth day of this honesty kick, no running from anyone or anything, including sudden responsibility for whatever I may have done, and it didn't seem to be fading. "I haven't seen him, Jaime," I said. "Haven't seen him for nearly a week. Hace una semana."

"Hmm," he said, his lips pressed tightly together, his smile suddenly gone. "Pues..." he said, and he lowered his head and moped away, shuffled toward the direction of the lake. I felt sorry for him, but only for a moment. I didn't really know him well enough.

I took the small bundle of letters into the kitchen and laid them on the table, trying not to look at them. I took the orange juice from the refrigerator, poured myself a tall glass, then before I sat took a sip. The juice was cold today, or at least getting so. The generator went out yesterday morning, thus the refrigeration. I at first thought I had let the fuel run empty again, but when I checked it the stick read full. During the afternoon lull at Daddy Rabbit's, Edelberto came down to give the thing a look.

"It has two problems," he said with that perfect English like his uncle Horacio. "A worn belt and a broken plug. Simple to fix." Those were indeed simple problems, problems that even someone not a poet and not a mechanic, someone having grown up in Aiken under the tutelage of a mechanic like my father, should be able to recognize and fix.

I have been getting lazy. Yes, having Gonzalo around the last seven years or so has made me at least mechanically lazy. I'll have to watch that.

Edelberto, with his thin, pliers-like fingers, his eyes that in their intensity spoke confident concentration, had both the belt and the plug replaced and repaired in a matter of minutes.

At least mentally, things didn't necessarily seem to be fleeing me. I had made a good choice in hiring him.

I placed the glass of juice on the table, then sat. I picked the stack of envelopes up and eyes averted tapped them on the table to straighten them, like you'd do preparing to shuffle a deck of cards. When they were in order, I set them back on the table face-down, addresses hidden, and began to go through them, turning up one at a time. I always go through the mail that way. Perhaps it's the suspense, at times (though of course not lately) it may for this *norteamericano* be the best game in town.

The first letter appeared to be some correspondence from a new dry-goods supplier in Guatemala City, probably offering me a one-month discount if I'd buy from them. Having gotten a similar letter last week, I set it aside without opening it. I was quite content with my current suppliers.

The second was from Ohio, from my sister Rachel, and it was postmarked July 13th, over three weeks ago. It felt thin and light. When her letters are like that, they are almost always nothing more than necessary hellos, no real news. The kids are having a good summer, Sid shot an 81 at Indian Hills last week, and so forth. I appreciate such letters, vacuous or not. It's nice to know that wherever you've fled to, you're not forgotten. But at the moment such news could wait, and besides, I wasn't so sure I didn't want to be forgotten. I filed the envelope unopened next to the other.

A couple of business-related items fell next, and they seemed at a glance important enough to open and at least give cursory attention to. I did so, nothing worth relating here.

I paused to take a sip of juice, then returned to the envelopes. By feel of weight I figured there were only three or four left, but I didn't count to make sure. No suspense that way. I turned, and a letter from my sister Linda came next, postmarked July 18th. Letters from her were a bit more rare than those from Rachel, so I opened it. Its contents can be summarized simply. She and her husband Hap had decided not to split after all. But he had totaled their car, a fairly new Ford Taurus, silver, which she had felt good driving. He'd gotten his second DUI and was spending a month in rehab in lieu of eleven twenty-nine in the county jail. He had been away two weeks now, and she wasn't missing him. Despite the loss of the car, life was looking up.

This news from Linda was good, but it came somehow with a hint of disappointment. I can't explain it. Maybe, I thought, at some point I expected this part of the family, like the other, to be something more than an old, dry skin I was trying to shed. It seemed a lousy thing to think.

You want things to be clear cut, and they aren't.

Loud raps came suddenly from the front door, three rapid knocks that startled me and made me jerk to attention. "Señor 'opkins," a voice yelled hoarsely, and I recognized it immediately as that of police chief Horacio Quiñones. They, whoever they were, had finally come for me.

Justice, of a sort, knocking at my door, or at least hollering through it, a door that if I'd had the capability to I'd have locked and barred. "I must speak with you, Señor 'opkins," yelled Horacio Quiñones, our local voice of justice. "Now, *ahora mismo*. It's important."

"I'm not here, Horacio," I yelled back, keeping my seat, leaning forward a bit and with my hands gently and shakily grasping the table edges. For a second, as I had many times over the last five days, I wished I had armed myself, in the night helped myself to some of the dead Miguel's supply of rifles, shotguns, and pistols next door. I only wished it for a second, though. I really didn't want to kill anyone else, least of all the uncle of my new employee Edelberto, who, again, was looking as if he would work out very well in his new job.

"You joke," Horacio yelled, and it seemed his voice suddenly came from somewhere closer. He certainly hadn't entered through the door, I'd have heard its slight squeak. Perhaps he had moved over in front of the window, where his mailman brother had stood just a few moments earlier. "But this is a serious matter, Jerry," he said. I couldn't remember the last time he'd called me by my first name. When he did it, though, it was something impressive. He pronounced the "j" the way we would up north, not as the "ch" so much more natural to a speaker of his native Spanish. "You must allow me to enter," he said. "This is an important matter, Jerry."

"Are you alone?" I asked, still seated at the table, still holding on to it.

"I am alone," he answered. "You have my word."

That was good enough for me. But, in the end, it had to be. "Come on in, Horacio," I said, and I could hear the resignation in my voice, though as I heard it I vowed to myself that I would not let such an emotion show again. I would be proud of who I was, where I'd come from, who I'd become. "It's not locked," I said. "I'm in the kitchen."

The door creaked open. Light footsteps moved behind me, came louder, closer. Despite Horacio's assurance that he was alone, I braced myself for the worst. For rough and painful handling by the two or more of them, for a scuffling ending in my face squashed unforgivingly to the floor and my hands cuffed harshly behind my back.

For, if not that, a single quick shot to the back of my head, a blast of a shot ending it all, ending it all more quickly and painlessly than even Uncle Fred's Quick Liquid Rat Poison ever could have, than anything I could imagine ever could have.

I wanted to trust Horacio, but then I'd wanted to trust Miguel, too.

I should say this now, and if anything redeems me this may be it:

Sometimes I think I should be more trusting of people who I've known for years and who for all that time, even though we may not know each other well, have claimed to be my friend.

"I know you, Jerry," Horacio said from over my shoulder. "You have been worried through the last few days."

"Are you alone?" I said.

"I said I was, and I am."

"What about your friend the Colonel."

"Oh, I have spoken with him, as I am certain you have imagined."

I let go of the table, stretched my shoulders back as if trying to appear nonchalant, and turned my head back toward him. He was dressed in the same military-style clothing as always, looked the same genuine, harmless man he had when I'd first met him slightly more than seven years ago, as he had always when I'd seen him so rarely since.

"Yes, Señor Quiñones," I said. "As you say, I've imagined you and our Colonel trying to decide what to do with me. You must know, of course, that I'm aware of Miguel Romero's role in the death of my friend Gonzalo." I nodded toward the other chair, the chair normally Nati's. "Please sit," I said. "Unless you have somewhere else more important you need to be."

"Yes," Horacio said, and he pulled the chair from the table and took it. He placed his hands gently on the table before us. I'd never noticed his hands. They appeared at once both gentle in their movements and rough in their thick, pink scars, scars of whatever war I had always until now been able to avoid being a part of. Hands so suddenly and startlingly rough and foreign in the scars they carried.

"And I guess you know," I said feeling somewhat humbled by those hands, "I guess you know I was there in the country when Miguel died, that some people might even say I was the one who killed him."

"That is why I have come," Horacio said. "And I apologize that I have not come before now, but intrusions have prevented it. There are certain bureaucracies I must deal with. Of course you understand."

"And you've talked with Aguilera?"

"We have spoken, yes. And we have decided that for the time being justice has been done We will not speak of *Señor* Romero again, you and I. It is an arrangement that you and I, as friends, must make between us."

I had spent the better part of a week losing sleep, losing Daddy Rabbit's-type productivity preparing myself to accept whatever punishment I as a murderer here in Guatemala might be due. That my killing of Miguel might be considered something just had never occurred to me. A pack of my cigarettes lay next to my juice, lay left from the night before, and I offered one to Horacio. He refused, and I lit one for myself.

"What will this cost me?" I asked him, an appropriate question, I thought.

"That is of course a thing you must ask. All I can say is now, nothing."

"Now," I said. "What about later, what about tomorrow?"

"I cannot say anything about later."

I took a drag from my cigarette and held it in. Sometimes in life you come across a situation in which all the experience in the world can't guide you. All I could think to do was assent, agree to keep quiet, to make no public mention of Miguel's responsibility for Gonzalo's death, to look no further into whoever else may have been involved in it, whatever goddamned inane reasons they'd had to kill him. All I could do was tacitly agree that my own silence would likely not be payment enough for the silence others would keep about me. That, finally, I may still owe somebody something, and that one day that somebody might come to collect. I exhaled, no relief.

"I have some orange juice if you'd like some," I said to Horacio. "It's not very cold, but thanks to your nephew Edelberto it's colder than it was this time yesterday."

"He is a fine young man. I told you that." Horacio blinked, and with his strangely rough right hand he rubbed his cheek. "This matter between us is closed now, wouldn't you agree?"

"I suppose I would," I answered, relieved, ashamed, frightened, not. Just myself.

Horacio smiled, shook his head no to the juice, stood, and left.

This was some reprieve I had won.

* * *

After Horacio closed the door behind him, after I heard the latch click shut, with an ambivalence I returned to my short stack of envelopes. Again, three or four left. I would force myself to give each my full attention. The next one, though, then the one after that, were not addressed to me, but rather to the owner of a bakery across *la avenida* from Daddy Rabbit's. Jaime, despite appearances and efforts, really isn't much of a mailman.

I placed those two with the letter from Rachel, all to be dealt with later. That left one, no counting necessary. Would it be from Jane? Of my sisters, she was the one I'd most like to hear from. Of course the one, after all, I most admire. Maybe for her poetic tendencies, which I have to envy, maybe for something else, something more ephemeral that I can't define. The letter could be from Jane.

Would it be from Audrey, though? I normally only heard from her some time soon after Moses's birthdays. She'd send me the latest picture, bring me up to date on the past year's news. I'd already gotten the most recent expected letter, a couple of months back. She had done well lately, still working as a bookkeeper for that friend of our old landlord. In that last letter she'd spoken of marrying, not the friend, but his younger brother. *He's a good man,* she'd said, *owns his own business.* Audrey was still alive, then, still growing. But I felt envy, had to, felt jealous of the man who so many years after I'd fled had taken my place, who now my son, mine, would be spending so much time with. Still, maybe, maybe correspondence between me and Audrey would become, if not more regular, at least more frequent. I could come to know young Moses.

Of course, the last letter would most likely be nothing of any import, if it was indeed for me at all. I turned it over, looked, recognized it as coming from Stevie's law firm, and opened it. His name, the Lubbers name, now came second on the letterhead, not third as it had in the letter I'd received just a couple of months before.

The contents of the letter from Stevie's law firm can be summarized thus:

The Pleasant Hill Lake Nuclear Weapons Facility was now an "Environment and Technology Site." And Stevie's law firm had decided not to pursue the suit against it and the Department of Energy. Not enough evidence. No clear enough connection between the company's waste and any death and disease downstream.

Oh, well, I thought. It wouldn't be the first time someone who shouldn't have had gotten off the hook.

I thought that, laughed at it oh so uncomfortably, then went up to the bed and took a nap.

Sleep came easy, something I can't explain.

I'm awake now, obviously. It's dark outside, but light in, thanks to Edelberto. Nati should be coming in soon, coming home. That's good. I miss her.

I have been writing. Finishing, I realize, this account. I've decided it will not be a part of the Hopkins family journals. It's too rambling, irreverent, self-conscious. It would be out of place there. Perhaps I've known that all along. Still, sometimes there are simply things inside a person that have to find their way out. So, here.

I've said that I may have been addressing this account to my sister Jane as much as to anybody. Years ago, the night before Audrey and I left Columbus, Jane told me to write. And, again, write I have, writer or not, poet or not. I think—no, I *know*—I'll send these pages to her. She'll read them, and Jane, she'll know what to do with them.

I'm putting this pen down now, picking up another, though parts of this story I've told bother me. I still don't know, for example, exactly how Gonzalo died, or precisely why, for that matter. I wish I could understand why people in my adopted country, in power or out, so often treat each other in the way they do.

And Audrey was in my story, was a great part of it for a long while. Then abruptly she disappeared. She faded out without a word to say for herself, stripped by my imperfect memory of the opportunity to offer her side of our story in its last days. I want to offer an excuse, to explain why I've forgotten so much about her, especially near the end. I won't, though, I don't really have one. But I will say this:

I would apologize to her if she were here.

So I hold a few discomforts. But it's time, I guess, I put them aside. I haven't made an entry in my section of the Hopkins family journals since the fourth of July, since I began devoting my time and energy to telling my own story instead of my family's. There's an empty page in them, a page waiting for an *August 5, 1992*, to be written in my hand across its first line, a *Gerard Manley Hopkins* to be written likewise across the bottom. An empty page, and more pages following, with lines and spaces all waiting to be filled...

But wait. Something's still not quite right.

It seems a postscript might be in order:

When I began writing this story of "my life so far," Gonzalo had just that day disappeared, though at the time, you'll recall, I hadn't assumed him to be missing, rather just doing his stint in the civil patrols. But as I wrote, the story of his murder, and of my final reaction to it with all its horrible consequences out there in Miguel's country *villa*, became as much a part of this account as all that came before.

This timing seems to me quite a coincidence, maybe too much of one. I'm not certain what to make of such things. But thinking back to my old neighbor Norma, Norma of the lisp and the rat dog Red, I have to wonder, faithful or not, if it might thimply be God, talking to me thith time.

THE AUTHOR

Jeff Lodge was born in Decatur, Illinois, in 1952. He attended Ohio State University and received a B.A. in English from the University of Arizona in Tucson in 1992, where he studied fiction writing with Robert Houston, Jonathan Penner, and Alan Harrington. He received an M.F.A. in creative writing from Virginia Commonwealth University in Richmond, where he studied with Tom De Haven, Paule Marshall, and poet Larry Levis. He has taught at Virginia Commonwealth University, John Tyler Community College and the University of Richmond. He lives in Richmond with his wife, Tamara Carter, and has recently completed a second novel.

THE SERIES

The White Pine Press New American Voices Series was established in 1996 in response to dramatic changes in the book industry that made it more and more difficult for first-time novelists to find a publisher. We believe that our literary heritage must continue to grow and that it must be vast enough to encompass the tremendous variety of writing from the Americas. Readers must be given the opportunity to hear vibrant, new voices. It is the intent of the series to present first novels that not only entertain but that also offer insights into our world and ourselves.

AMERICAN FICTION FROM WHITE PINE PRESS

BLACK FLAMES
A Novel by Daniel Pearlman
192 pages $14.00

I SAW A MAN HIT HIS WIFE
Stories by Mark Greenside
224 pages $14.00

THE VOICE OF MANUSH
A Novel by Victor Walter
276 pages $14.00

GOLDSMITH'S RETURN
A Novel by Terry Richard Bazes
288 pages $14.00

LIMBO
A Novel by Dixie Salazar
200 pages $14.00

WAY BELOW E
Stories by Patrick J. Murphy
230 pages $14.00

PRAYERS FOR THE DEAD
Stories by Dennis Vannatta
196 pages $14.00

THIS TIME, THIS PLACE
Stories by Dennis Vannatta
186 pages $10.00

DREAMS OF DISTANT LIVES
Stories by Lee K. Abbott
206 pages $10.00

CROSSING WYOMING
A Novel by David Romtvedt
263 pages $12.00

EXTRAVAGANZA
A Novel by Gordon Lish
190 pages $10.00

OTHER FICTION FROM WHITE PINE PRESS

REMAKING A LOST HARMONY
Fiction from the Hispanic Caribbean
250 pages $17.00

MYTHS AND VOICES
Contemporary Canadian Fiction
420 pages $17.00

THE SNOWY ROAD
Contemporary Korean Fiction
167 pages $12.00

HAPPINESS
Stories by Marjorie Agosín
238 pages $14.00

RAIN AND OTHER FICTIONS
Stories by Maurice Kenny
94 pages $8.00

FALLING THROUGH THE CRACKS
Stories by Julio Ricci
82 pages $8.00

THE DAY I BEGAN MY STUDIES IN PHILOSOPHY
Stories by Margareta Ekström
98 pages $9.00

HERMAN
A Novel by Lars Saabye Christensen
186 pages $12.00

THE JOKER
A Novel by Lars Saabye Christensen
200 pages $10.00

AN OCCASION OF SIN
Stories by John Montague
200 pages $12.00

THE SECRET WEAVERS SERIES
Series Editor: Marjorie Agosín

Dedicated to bringing the rich and varied writing by Latin American women to the English-speaking audience.

White Pine Press is a non-profit publishing house dedicated to enriching our literary heritage; promoting cultural awareness, understanding, and respect; and, through literature, addressing social and human rights issues. This mission is accomplished by discovering, producing, and marketing to a diverse circle of readers exceptional works of poetry, fiction, non-fiction, and literature in translation from around the world. Through White Pine Press, authors' voices reach out across cultural, ethnic, and gender boundaries to educate and to entertain.

To insure that these voices are heard as widely as possible, White Pine Press arranges author reading tours and speaking engagements at various colleges, universities, organizations, and bookstores throughout the country. White Pine Press works with colleges and public schools to enrich curricula and promotes discussion in the media. Through these efforts, literature extends beyond the books to make a difference in a rapidly changing world.

As a non-profit organization, White Pine Press depends on support from individuals, foundations, and government agencies to bring you this literature that matters—work that might not be published by profit-driven publishing houses. Our grateful thanks to the many individuals who support this effort as Friends of White Pine Press and to the following organizations: Amter Foundation, Ford Foundation, Korean Culture and Arts Foundation, Lannan Foundation, Lila Wallace-Reader's Digest Fund, Margaret L. Wendt Foundation, Mellon Foundation, National Endowment for the Arts, New York State Council on the Arts, Trubar Foundation, Witter Bynner Foundation, the Slovenian Ministry of Culture, The U.S.-Mexico Fund for Culture, and Wellesley College.

Please support White Pine Press' efforts to present voices that promote cultural awareness and increase understanding and respect among diverse populations of the world. Tax-deductible donations can be made to:

White Pine Press
10 Village Square · Fredonia, NY 14063